"WORLDS FOR SALE!"

That was the startling cry that electrified Dane Thorson of the space-trader *Solar Queen*. It was his first trip and the cosmic auction was taking place at an isolated port of call, far out in the Milky Way.

Who'll buy this newly discovered planet? The data on it sealed—you may be getting a radioactive desert, you may be buying a fabulous empire, or you may be stuck with an untracked unconquerable jungle! And Dane and his fellow spacemen took the risk. They bought a planet, sight unseen, whose ominous name was . . . Limbo!

SARGASSO
OF SPACE

by
Andre Norton

ace books
A Division of Charter Communications Inc.
A GROSSET & DUNLAP COMPANY
360 Park Avenue South
New York, New York 10010

SARGASSO OF SPACE

An ACE Book, by arrangement with Gnome Press, Inc.

Cover art by Don Brautigan

Fifth Ace printing: July 1978

Printed in U.S.A.

1 THE SOLAR QUEEN

THE LANKY, very young man in the ill-fitting Trader's tunic tried to stretch the cramp out of his long legs. You'd think, Dane Thorson considered the point with a certain amount of irritation, the men who designed these under-surface transcontinental cars would take into mind that there would be tall passengers—not just midgets—using them. Not for the first time he wished that he could have used air transport. But he had only to finger the money belt, too flat about his middle, to remember who and what he was—a recruit new to the Service, without a ship or backer.

There was his muster pay from Training Pool, and a thin pad of crumpled credit slips which remained from the sale of all those belongings which could not follow him into space. And he had his minimum kit—that was the total sum of his possessions—except for that slender wafer of metal, notched and incised with a code beyond his reading, which would be his passport to what he determined was going to be a brighter future.

Not that he should question the luck he had had so far, Dane told himself firmly. After all it wasn't every boy from a Federation Home who could get an appointment to the Pool and emerge ten years later an apprentice-Cargo-Master ready for ship assignment off world. Even recalling the stiff examinations of the past few weeks could set him to squirming now. Basic mechanics, astrogation grounding, and then the more severe testing in his own specialization—cargo handling, stowage, trade procedure, Galactic markets, Extraterrestrial psychology, and all the other items he had had to try and cram into his skull until he sometimes thought that he had nothing but bits and patches which he would never be able to sort into common sense. Not only had the course been tough, but he had been bucking the new trend in selection, too. Most of his classmates were from Service families—they had grown up in Trade.

Dane frowned at the back of the seat before him. Wasn't Trade becoming more and more a closed clan? Sons followed fathers or brothers into the Service—it was increasingly difficult for a man without connections to get an appointment to the Pool. His luck had been good there——

Look at Sands, he had two older brothers, an uncle and a cousin all with Inter-Solar. And he never let anyone forget it either. Just let an apprentice get assigned into one of the big Companies and he was set for the rest of his life. The Companies had regular runs from one system to another. Their employees were always sure of a steady berth, you could buy Company stock. There were pensions and adminis-

trative jobs when you had to quit space—if you'd
shown any promise. They had the cream of Trade—
Inter-Solar, The Combine, Deneb-Galactic, Falworth-Ignesti——

Dane blinked at the tela-screen at eye level at the
far end of the bullet-shaped car—not really seeing
the commercial which at that moment was singing
the praises of a Falworth-Ignesti import. It all depended on the Psycho. He patted his money belt
again to be sure of the safety of his ID wafer, sealed
into its most secret pocket.

The commercial faded into the red bar announcing
a station. Dane waited for the faint jar which signalized the end of his two-hour trip. He was glad to
be free of the projectile, able to drag his kit bag out of
the mound of luggage from the van.

Most of his fellow travelers were Trade men. But
few of them sported Company badges. The majority
were drifters or Free Traders, men who either from
faults of temperament or other reasons could not
find a niche in the large parental organizations, but
shipped out on one independent spacer or another,
the bottom layer of the Trade world.

Dane shouldered his bag into the lift which swept
him up to ground level and out into the sunshine of a
baking southwestern summer day. He lingered on
the concrete apron which rimmed this side of the
take-off Field, looking out over its pitted and blasted
surface at the rows of cradles which held those ships
now readying for flight. He had scant attention for
the stubby interplanetary traders, the Martian and
Asteroid lines, the dull dark ships which plowed out
to Saturn's and Jupiter's moons. What he wanted lay

beyond—the star ships—their sleek sides newly sprayed against dust friction, the soil of strange worlds perhaps still clinging to their standing fins.

"Well, if it isn't the Viking! Hunting for your long boat, Dane?"

Only someone who knew Dane very well could have read the real meaning in that twitch of his lower lip. When he turned to face the speaker his expression was under its usual tight control.

Artur Sands had assumed the swagger of a hundred voyage man, which contrasted oddly, Dane was pleased to note, with his too shiny boots and unworn tunic. But as ever the other's poise aroused his own secret resentment. And Artur was heading his usual chorus of followers too, Ricki Warren and Hanlaf Bauta.

"Just come in, Viking? Haven't tried your luck yet, I take it? Neither have we. So let's go together to learn the worst."

Dane hesitated. The last thing in the world he wanted to do was to face the Psycho in Artur Sands' company. To him the other's supreme self-confidence was somewhat unnerving. Sands expected the best, and judging from various incidents at the Pool, what Artur expected he usually got.

On the other hand Dane had often good reason to worry about the future. And if he were going to have hard luck now he would rather learn it without witnesses. But there was no getting rid of Artur he realized. So philosophically he checked his kit while the others waited impatiently.

They had come by air—the best was none too good for Artur and his crowd. Why hadn't they been to the cargo department assignment Psycho before this? Why had they waited the extra hour—or had they spent their last truly free time sightseeing? Surely—Dane knew a little lift of heart at the thought—it couldn't be that *they* were dubious about the machine's answer too?

But that hope was quenched as he joined them in time to hear Artur expound his favorite theme.

"The machine is impartial! That's just the comet dust they feed you back at the Pool. Sure, we know the story they set up—that a man has to be fitted by temperament and background to his job, that each ship had to carry a well integrated crew— But that's all moon gas! When Inter-Solar wants a man, they get him—and no Psycho fits him into their ships if they don't want him! That's for the guys who don't know how to fire the right jets—or haven't brains enough to look around for good berths. I'm not worrying about being stuck on some starving Free Trader on the fringe——"

Ricki and Hanlaf were swallowing every word of that. Dane didn't want to. His belief in the incorruptibility of the Psycho was the one thing he had clung to during the past few weeks when Artur and those like him had strutted about the Pool confident about their speedy transition to the higher levels of Trade.

He had preferred to believe that the official statements were correct, that a machine, a collection of impulses and relays which could be in no way influenced, decided the fate of all who applied for assignment to off-world ships. He wanted to believe that when he fed his ID plate into the Psycho at the star port here it would make no difference that he was an orphan without kin in the Service, that the flatness of his money belt could not turn or twist a decision which would be based only on his knowledge, his past record at the Pool, his temperament and potentialities.

But doubt had been planted and it was that lack of faith which worked on him now, slowing his pace as they approached the assignment room. On the other hand Dane had no intention of allowing Artur or either of his satellites to guess he was bothered.

So a stubborn pride pushed him forward to be the first of the four to fit his ID into the waiting slot. His fingers twitched to snatch it back again before it disappeared, but he controlled that impulse and stood aside for Artur.

The Psycho was nothing but a box, a square of solid metal—or so it looked to the waiting apprentices. And that wait might have been easier, Dane speculated, had they been able to watch the complicated processes inside the bulk, could have seen how those lines and notches incised on their plates were assessed, matched, paired, until a ship now in port and seeking apprentices was found for them.

Long voyaging for small crews sealed into star spacers, with little chance for recreation or amusement, had created many horrible personnel problems in the past. Some tragic cases were now required reading in the "History of Trade" courses at the Pool. Then came the Psycho and through its impersonal selection the right men were sent to the right ships, fitted into the type of work, the type of crew where they could function best with the least friction. No one at the Pool had told them how the Psycho worked—or how it could actually read an ID strip. But when the machine decided, its decision was final and the verdict was recorded—there was no appeal.

That was what they had been taught, what Dane had always accepted as fact, and how could it be wrong?

His thoughts were interrupted by a gong note from the machine, one ID strip had been returned, with a new line on its surface. Artur pounced. A moment later his triumph was open.

"Inter-Solar's *Star Runner!* Knew you wouldn't let the old man down, boy!" He patted the flat top of the Psycho patronizingly. "Didn't I tell you how it would work for me?"

Ricki nodded his head eagerly and Hanlaf went so far as to slap Artur on the back. Sands was the magician who had successfully pulled off a trick.

The next two sounds of the gong came almost together, as the strips clicked in the holder on top of one another. Ricki and Hanlaf scooped them up. There was disappointment on Ricki's face.

"Martian-Terran Incorporated—the *Venturer*," he read aloud. And Dane noted that the hand with which he tucked his ID into his belt was shaking. Not for Ricki the far stars and big adventures, but a small berth in a crowded planetary service where there was little chance for fame or fortune.

"The Combine's *Deneb Warrior!*" Hanlaf was openly exultant, paying no attention to Ricki's announcement.

"Shake, enemy!" Artur held out his hand with a

grin. He, too, ignored Ricki as if his late close companion had been removed bodily from their midst by the decision of the Psycho.

"Put her there, rival!" Hanlaf had been completely shaken out of his usual subservience by this amazing good fortune.

The Combine was big, big enough to offer a challenge to Inter-Solar these past two years. They had copped a Federation mail contract from under I-S's nose and pounded through, at least one monopolistic concession on an inner system's route. Artur and his former follower might never meet in open friendship again. But at the present their mutual luck in getting posts in the Companies was all that mattered.

Dane continued to wait for the Psycho to answer him. Was it possible for an ID to jam somewhere in the interior of that box? Should he hunt for someone in authority and ask a question or two? His strip had been the first to go in—but it was not coming out. And Artur was waking up to that fact——

"Well, well, no ship for the Viking? Maybe they haven't got one to fit your particular scrambled talents, big boy——"

Could that be true, Dane hazarded? Maybe no ship now in the Port cradles needed the type of service his strip said he had to offer. Did that mean that he would have to stay right here until such a ship came in?

It was as if Artur could read his thoughts. Sands' grin changed from one of triumph to a malicious half-sneer.

"What did I tell you?" he demanded. "Viking

8

doesn't know the right people. Going to bring in your kit and camp out until Psycho breaks down and gives you an answer?''

Hanlaf was impatient. His self-confidence had been given a vast jolt towards independence, so that now he dared to question Artur.

''I'm starved,'' he announced. ''Let's mess—and then look up our ships———''

Artur shook his head. ''Give it a minute or two. I want to see if the Viking gets his long boat—if it's in dock now———''

Dane could only do what he had done many times before, pretend that this did not matter, that Artur and his followers meant nothing. But was the machine functioning, or had his ID been lost somewhere within its mysterious interior? Had Artur not been there, watching him with that irritating amusement, Dane would have gone to find help.

Hanlaf started to walk away and Ricki was already at the door, as if *his* assignment had removed him forever from the ranks of those who mattered—when the gong sounded for the fourth time. With a speed the average observer would not have credited to him, Dane moved. His hands dashed under Artur's fingers and caught the ID before the smaller youth could grab it.

There was no bright line of a Company insignia on it—Dane's first glance told him that. Was—was he going to be confined to the system—follow in Ricki's uninspired wake?

But, no, there was a star on it right enough—the star which granted him the Galaxy—and by that emblem the name of a ship—not a Company but a ship—the *Solar Queen*. It took a long instant for that to make sense, though he had never considered himself a slow thinker.

A ship's name only—a Free Trader! One of the roving, exploring spacers which plied lanes too dangerous, too new, too lacking in quick profits to attract the Companies. Part of the Trade Service right enough, and the uninitiated thought of them as romantic. But Dane knew a pinched sinking in his middle. Free Trade was almost a dead end for the ambitious. Even the instructors at the Pool had skimmed over that angle in the lectures, as carefully as the students were briefed. Free Trade was too often a gamble with death, with plague, with hostile alien races. You could lose not only your profit and your ship, but your life. And the Free Traders rated close to the bottom of the scale in the Service. Why, even Ricki's appointment would be hailed by any apprentice as better than this!

He should have been prepared for Artur's hand over his shoulder to snatch the ID, for the other's quick appraisement of his shame.

"Free Trader!"

It seemed to Dane that Sands' voice rang out as loudly as the telecast.

Ricki paused in his retreat and stared. Hanlaf allowed himself a snicker and Artur laughed.

"So that's how *your* pattern reads, big boy? You're to be a viking of space—a Columbus of the star lanes—a far rover! How's your blaster aim, man? And hadn't you better go back for a refresher in X-Tee contacts? Free Traders don't see much of civilization, you know. Come on, boys," he turned

10

to the other two, "we've got to treat the Viking to a super-spread meal, he'll be on conrations for the rest of his life no doubt." His grip tightened on Dane's arm. And, though his captive might easily have twisted free, the prisoner knew that he could better save face and dignity by going along with the plan and bottling down all signs of anger.

Sure—maybe the Free Traders did not rate so high in the Service, maybe few of them swanked around the big ports as did the Company men. But there had been plenty of fortunes made in the outer reaches and no one could deny that a Free Trader got around. Artur's attitude set Dane's inborn stubbornness to finding the good in the future. His spirit had hit bottom during the second when he had read his assignment, now it was rising again.

There were no strict caste lines in Trade, the divisions were not by rank but by employer. The large dining room at the Port was open to every man wearing the tunic of active service. Most of the Companies maintained their own sections there, their employees paying with vouchers. But transients and newly assigned men who had not yet joined their ships drifted together among the tables by the door.

Dane got to an empty one first and triggered the check button. He might be a Free Trader but this party was his, he was not going to eat any meal provided by Artur—even if this gesture swept away most of his credits.

They had some minutes to look around them after dialing for meals. A short distance away a man wearing the lightning flash badge of a Com-Tech was arising from the table. He left two companions still methodically chewing as he went off, his wide chest—that of a second or third generation Martian colonist—unmistakable, though his features were those of a Terran Oriental.

The two he left behind were both apprentices. One bore on his tunic the chart insignia of an astrogator-to-be and the other an engineer's cogwheel. It was the latter who caught and held Dane's gaze.

The cargo-apprentice thought that never before had he seen such a handsome, daredevil face. The crisp black hair which framed the finely cut, space tanned features, was cropped short, but not short enough to hide a wave. The heavy lidded eyes were dark, and a little amused smile held more than a hint of cynicism as it quirked the corners of his too-perfectly cut lips. He was a Video idea of the heroic space man and Dane disliked him on sight.

But the perfect one's companion was as rough hewn as he was faceted. His naturally brown skin could have taken no deeper tan for he was a Negro. And he was talking animatedly about something which sparked languid answers from the budding engineer.

Dane's attention was brought back to his own table by a waspish sting from Artur.

"*Solar Queen*," he spoke the name much too loudly to suit Dane. "A Free Trader. Well, you'll get to see life, Viking, that you will. At any rate we can continue to speak to you—since you aren't on any rival listing——"

Dane achieved something close to a smile. "That's big-minded of you, Sands. How dare I

12

complain if an Inter-Solar man is willing to acknowledge my existence?''

Ricki broke in. ''That's dangerous—the Free Trade, I mean——''

But Artur frowned. To a dangerous trade some glamor might still cling, and he refused to allow that. ''Oh, not all the Free Traders are explorers or fringe system men, Ricki. Some have regular runs among the poorer planets where it doesn't pay the Companies to operate. Dane'll probably find himself on a back and forth job between a couple of dome-citied worlds where he can't even take a breath outside his helmet——''

Which is just what you would like, isn't it? Dane concluded inside. The picture isn't black enough to suit you yet, is it, Sands? And for a second or two he wondered why Sands got pleasure out of riding him.

''Yes—'' Ricki subsided fast. But Dane was aware that his eyes continued to watch the new Free Trader wistfully.

''Here's to Trade anyway you have it!'' Artur raised his mug with a theatrical gesture. ''Best of luck to the *Solar Queen*. You'll probably need it, Viking.''

Dane was stung anew. ''I don't know about that, Sands. Free Traders have made big strikes. And the gamble——''

''That's just it, old man, the gamble! And the chips can fall down as well as up. For one Free Trader who has made a stroke, there're a hundred or so who can't pay their Field fees. Too bad you didn't have some pull with the powers-that-be.''

Dane had had enough. He pushed back from the

13

table and looked at Artur straightly. "I'm going where the Psycho assigned me," he said steadily. "All this talk about Free Trading being so tough may be just meteor light. Give us both a year in space, Sands, and then you can talk——"

Artur laughed. "Sure—give me a year with Inter-Solar and you a year in that broken down bucket. I'll buy the dinner next time, Viking, you won't have credits enough to settle the bill—I'll wager an extra ten on that. Now," he glanced at his watch, "I'm going to have a look at the *Star Runner*. Any of you care to join me?"

It seemed that Ricki and Hanlaf would, at least they arose with dispatch to join him. But Dane remained where he was, finishing the last of a very good dinner, certain that it would be a long time before he tasted its like again. He had, he hoped, put up a good front and he was heartily tired of Sands.

But he was not left to his own company. Someone slipped into Ricki's chair across the table and spoke:

"You for the *Solar Queen*, man?"

Dane's head snapped up. Was this to be more of Artur's pleasantries? But now he was looking at the open face of the astrogator-apprentice from the neighboring table. He lost part of his bristling antagonism.

"Just been assigned to her." He passed his ID across to the other.

"Dane Thorson," the other read aloud. "I am Rip Shannon—Ripley Shannon if you wish to be formal. And," he beckoned to the Video hero, "this is Ali Kamil. We are both of the *Queen*. You are a cargo-apprentice," he ended with a statement rather than a question.

Dane nodded and then greeted Kamil, hoping that the stiffness he felt was not apparent in his voice or manner. He thought that the other looked him over too appraisingly, and that in some mysterious way he had been found wanting after the instant of swift measurement.

"We are going to the *Queen* now, come with us?" Rip's simple friendliness was warming and Dane agreed.

As they boarded the scooter which trundled down the length of the Field toward the distant cradles of the star ships, Rip kept up a flow of conversation and Dane warmed more and more to the big young man. Shannon was older, he must be in his last year of apprenticeship, and the newcomer was grateful for the scraps of information about the *Queen* and her present crew which were being passed along to him.

Compared to the big super ships of the Companies the *Solar Queen* was a negligible midget. She carried a crew of twelve, and each man was necessarily responsible for more than one set of duties—there were no air tight compartments of specialization aboard a Free Trader spacer.

"Got us a routine cargo haul to Naxos," Rip's soft voice continued. "From there," he shrugged, "it may be anywhere——"

"Except back to Terra," Kamil's crisper tone cut in. "Better say goodbye to home for a long while, Thorson. We won't be hitting this lane for some time. Only came in on this voyage because we had a special run and that doesn't happen once in ten years or more.'' Dane thought that the other was getting some obscure pleasure in voicing that piece of daunting information.

The scooter rounded the first of the towering cradles. Here were the Company ships in their private docks, their needle points lifted to the sky, cargoes being loaded, activity webbing them. Dane stared in spite of himself, but he did not turn his head to keep them in sight as the scooter steered to the left and made for the other line of berths, not so well filled, where the half dozen smaller Free Trade ships stood awaiting blast off. And somehow he was not surprised when they drew up at the foot of the ramp leading to the most battered one.

But there was affection and honest pride in Rip's voice as he announced.

''There she is, man, the best trading spacer along the lanes. She's a real lady, is the *Queen!*''

2 WORLDS FOR SALE

DANE STEPPED inside the Cargo-Master's office cabin. The man who sat there, surrounded by files of microtape and all the other apparatus of an experienced trader, was not at all what he expected. Those Masters who had given lectures at the Pool had been sleek, well groomed men, their outward shells differing little from the successful earthbound executive. It had been difficult to associate some of them with space at all.

But more than J. Van Rycke's uniform proclaimed him of the Service. His thinning hair was white-blond, his broad face reddened rather than tanned. And he was a big man—though not in fatty tissue, but solid bulk. He occupied every inch of his cushioned seat, eyeing Dane with a sleepy indifference, an attitude shared by a large tiger-striped tom cat who sprawled across a third of the limited desk space.

Dane saluted. "Apprentice-Cargo-Master Thorson come aboard, sir," he rapped out with the snap approved by Pool officers, laying his ID on the desk when his new commander made no attempt to reach for it.

"Thorson—" the bass voice seemingly rumbled not from the broad chest but from deep in the barrel body facing him. "First voyage?"

"Yes, sir."

The cat blinked and yawned, but Van Rycke's measuring stare did not change. Then——

"Better report to the Captain and sign on." There was no other greeting.

A little at a loss Dane climbed on to the control section. He flattened against the wall of the narrow corridor as another officer swung along behind him at a hurried pace. It was the Com-tech who had been eating with Rip and Kamil.

"New?" The single word came from him with some of the same snap as the impulses in his communicators.

"Yes, sir. I'm to sign on——"

"Captain's office—next level," and he was gone.

Dane followed him at a more modest pace. It was true that the *Queen* was no giant of the spaceways, and she doubtless lacked a great many refinements and luxurious fittings which the Company ships boasted. But Dane, green as he was, appreciated the smartly kept interior of the ship. Her sides might be battered and she had a rakish, too worn appearance without—inside she was a smooth running, tight held vessel. He reached the next level and knocked at a half open panel. At an impatient order he entered.

For one dazed moment he felt as if he had stepped into the Terraport X-Tee Zoo. The walls of the confined space were a montage of pictures—but such pictures! Off-world animals he had seen, had heard described, overlapped others which were strictly culled from more gruesome nightmares. In a small swinging cage sat a blue creature which could only be an utterly impossible combination of toad—if toads had six legs, two of them ending in claws—and parrot. It leaned forward, gripped the cage bars with its claws, and calmly spat at him.

Fascinated, Dane stood rooted until a rasping bark aroused him.

"Well—what is it?"

Dane hastily averted his eyes from the blue horror and looked at the man who sat beneath its cage. Grizzled hair showed an inch or so beneath the Captain's winged cap. His harsh features had not been improved by a scar across one cheek, a seam which could only have been a blaster-blister. And his eyes were as cold and imperious as the pop ones of his blue captive.

Dane found his tongue. "Apprentice-Cargo-Master Thorson come aboard, sir," again he tendered the ID.

Captain Jellico caught it up impatiently. "First voyage?"

Once more Dane was forced to answer in the affirmative. It would have been, he thought bleakly, so much better had he been able to say "tenth."

At that moment the blue thing sirened an ear piercing shriek and the Captain swung back in his chair to strike the door of the cage a resounding slap which bounced its occupant into silence, if not better manners. Then he dropped the ID into the ship's recorder and punched the button. Dane dared to relax, it was official now, he was signed on as a crew member, he would not be booted off the *Queen*.

"Blast off at eighteen hours," the Captain told him. "Find your quarters."

"Yes, sir." He rightly took that for dismissal and saluted, glad to be out of Captain Jellico's zoo—even if only one inhabitant was living.

As he dropped down again to the cargo section, Dane wondered from what strange world the blue thing had come and why the Captain was so enamored of it that he carried it about in the *Queen*. As far as Dane could see it had no endearing qualities at all.

Whatever cargo the *Queen* had shipped for Naxos was already aboard. He saw the hatch seals in place as he passed the hold. So his department's duties were done for this port. He was free to explore the small cabin Rip Shannon had indicated was his and pack away in its lockers his few personal belongings.

At the Pool he had lived in a hammock and locker, to him the new quarters were a comfortable expansion. When the signal came to strap down for blast off, he was fast gaining the contentment Artur Sands had threatened to destroy.

They were space borne before Dane met the other members of the crew. In addition to Captain Jellico, the control station was manned by Steen Wilcox, a lean Scot in his early thirties who had served a hitch in the Galactic Survey before going into Trade, and now held a full rating as Astrogator. Then there was the Martian Com-Tech—Tang Ya—and Rip, the apprentice.

The engine-room section was an equal number, consisting of the Chief, Johan Stotz, a silent young man who appeared to have little interest save his engines (Dane gathered from Rip's scraps of information that Stotz was in his way a mechanical genius who could have had much better berths than the aging *Queen*, but chose to stay with the challenge she offered), and his apprentice—the immaculate, almost foppish Kamil. But, Dane soon knew, the *Queen* carried no dead weight and Kamil must—in spite of his airs and graces—be able to meet the exacting standards such a Chief as Stotz could set. The engine room staff was rounded out by a giant-dwarf combination, startling to see.

Karl Kosti, was a lumbering bear of a man, almost bovine, but as alert to his duties with the jets as a piece of perfectly working machinery. While around him buzzed his opposite number, a fly about a bull, the small Jasper Weeks, his thin face pallid with that bleach produced on Venus, a pallor not even the rays of space could color to a natural brown.

Dane's own fellows housed on the cargo level were a varied lot. There was Van Rycke himself, a superior so competent when it came to the matters of his own section that he might have been a computer. He kept Dane in a permanent state of awe, there appeared to be nothing concerning the fine points of Free Trade Van Rycke had ever missed hearing or learning, and, having once added any fact to his prodigious store of memories, it was embedded forever. But he had his soft spot, his enduring pride that as a Van Rycke he was one of a line stretching far back into the dim past when ships only plied the waters of a single planet, coming of a family which had been in Trade from the days of sails to the days of stars.

Two others who were partly of the cargo world

shared this section. The Medic, Craig Tau, and the Cook-Steward Frank Mura. Tau Dane met in the course of working hours now and then, but Mura kept so closely to his own quarters and labors that they seldom saw much of him.

In the meantime the new apprentice was kept busy, laboring in an infinitesimal space afforded him in the cargo office to check the rolls, being informally but mercilessly quizzed by Van Rycke and learning to his dismay what large gaps unfortunately existed in his training. Dane was speedily reduced to a humble wonder that Captain Jellico had ever shipped him at all—in spite of the assignment of the Psycho. It was too evident that in his present state of overwhelming ignorance he was more of a liability than an asset.

But Van Rycke was not just a machine of facts and figures, he was also a superb raconteur, a collector of legends who could keep the whole mess spellbound as he spun one of his tales. No one but he could pay such perfect tribute to the small details of the eerie story of the *New Hope*, that ship which had blasted off with refugees from the Martian rebellion, never to be sighted until a century later—the *New Hope* wandering forever in free fall, its dead lights glowing evilly red at its nose, its escape ports ominously sealed—the *New Hope* never boarded, never salvaged because it was only sighted by ships which were themselves in dire trouble, so that "to sight the *New Hope*" had become a synonym for the worst of luck.

Then there were the "Whisperers," whose siren voices were heard by those men who had been too long in space, and about whom a whole mythology had developed. Van Rycke could list the human demi-gods of the star lanes, too. Sanford Jones, the first man who had dared Galactic flight, whose lost ship had suddenly lashed out of Hyperspace, over a Sirius world three centuries after it had lifted from Terra, the mummified body of the pilot still at the frozen controls, Sanford Jones who now welcomed on board that misty "Comet" all spacemen who died with their magnetic boots on. Yes, in his way, Van Rycke made his new assistant free of more than one kind of space knowledge.

The voyage to Naxos was routine. And the frontier world where they set down at its end was enough like Terra to be unexciting too. Not that Dane got any planetside leave. Van Rycke put him in charge of the hustlers at the unloading. And the days he had spent poring over the hold charts suddenly paid off as he discovered that he could locate everything with surprising ease.

Van Rycke went off with the Captain. Upon their bargaining ability, their collective nose for trade, depended the next flight of the *Queen*. And no ship lingered in port longer than it took her to discharge one cargo and locate another.

Mid-afternoon of the second day found Dane unemployed. He was lounging a little dispiritedly by the crew hatch with Kosti. None of the *Queen's* men had gone into the sprawling frontier town half encircled by the bulbous trees with the red-yellow foliage, there was too much chance that they might be needed for cargo hustling, since the Field men were celebrating a local holiday and were not at their posts. Thus both Dane and the jetman witnessed the return of the hired scooter which tore down the field toward them at top speed.

It slewed around, raising more dust, and came to a skidding stop at the foot of the ramp. Captain Jellico leaped for that, almost reaching the hatch before Van Rycke had pried himself from behind the controls. And the Captain threw a single order at Kosti:

"Order assembly in the mess cabin!"

Dane stared back over the field, half expecting to see at least a squad of police in pursuit. The officers' return had smacked of the need for a quick getaway. But all he saw was his own superior ascending the ramp at his usual dignified pace. Only Van Rycke was whistling, a sign Dane had come to know meant that all was very well with the Dutchman's world. Whatever the Captain's news, the Cargo-Master considered it good.

As the latest and most junior member of the crew, Dane squeezed into the last small portion of room just inside the mess cabin door a few minutes later. From Tau to the usually absent Mura, the entire complement of the ship was present, their attention for Captain Jellico who sat at the head of the small table, moving his finger tips back and forth across the old blaster scar on his cheek.

"And what pot of gold has fallen into our hands this time, Captain?" That was Steen Wilcox asking the question which was in all their minds.

"Survey auction!" the words burst out of Jellico as if he simply could not restrain them any longer.

Somebody whistled, and someone else gasped. Dane blinked, he was too new to the game to understand at once. But when the full purport of the announcement burst upon him he knew a surge of red hot excitement. A Survey auction—a Free Trader got a chance at one of those maybe once in a lifetime. And that was how fortunes were made.

"Who's in town?" Engineer Stotz's eyes were narrowed, he was looking at the Captain almost accusingly.

Jellico shrugged. "All the usual. But it's been a long trip, and there are four Class D-s listed as up for bids——"

Dane calculated rapidly. The Companies would automatically scoop up the A and B listings—there would be tussles over the C-s. And four D-s—four newly discovered planets whose trading rights auctioned off under Federation law would come within range of the price Free Traders could raise. Would the *Queen* be able to enter the contest for one of them? A complete five- or ten-year monopoly on the rights of Trade with a just chartered world could make them all wealthy—if luck rode their jets!

"How much in the strong box?" Tau asked Van Rycke.

"When we pick up the voucher for this last load and pay our Field fees there'll be— But what about supplies, Frank?"

The thin little steward was visibly doing sums in his head. "Say a thousand for restocking—that gives us a good margin—unless we're in for a rim haul——"

"All right, Van, cutting out that thousand—what can we raise?" It was Jellico's turn to ask.

There was no need for the Cargo-Master to consult

his books, the figures were part of the amazing catalogue within his mind. "Twenty-five thousand—maybe six hundred more——"

There was a deflated silence. No Survey auctioneer would accept that amount. It was Wilcox who broke the quiet.

"Why are they having an auction here, anyway? Naxos is no Federation district planet."

It was queer, come to think of it, Dane agreed. He had never before heard of a trading auction being held on any world which was not at least a sector capitol.

"The Survey ship *Rimwold* has been reported too long overdue," Jellico's voice came flatly. "All available ships have been ordered to conclude business and get into space to quarter for her. This ship here—the *Griswold*—came in to the nearest planet to hold auction. It's some kind of legal rocket wash——"

Van Rycke's broad finger tips drummed on the table top. "There are Company agents here. On the other hand there are only two other independent Traders in port. Unless another planets before sixteen hours today, we have four worlds to share between the three of us. The Companies don't want D-s—their agents have definite orders not to bid for them."

"Look here, sir," that was Rip. "In that twenty-five thousand—did you include the pay-roll?"

When Van Rycke shook his head Dane guessed what Rip was about to suggest. And for a moment he knew resentment. To be asked to throw one's voyage earnings into a wild gamble—and that was what would happen he was sure—was pretty tough. He wouldn't have the courage to vote no against it either——

"With the pay-roll in?" Tau's soft, unaccented voice questioned.

"About thirty-eight thousand—"

"Pretty lean for a Survey auction," Wilcox was openly dubious.

"Miracles have happened," Tang Ya pointed out. "I say—try it. If we lose we're not any the worse——"

It was agreed by a hand vote, no one dissenting, that the crew of the *Queen* would add their pay to the reserve—sharing in proportion to the sum they had surrendered in any profits to come. Van Rycke by common consent was appointed the bidder. But none of them would have willingly stayed away from the scene of action and Captain Jellico agreed to hire a Field guard as they left the ship in a body to try their luck.

The dusk of Naxos was early, the air away from the fuel vapors of the Field, scented with growing things, almost too much so to suit their Terran nostrils. It was a typical frontier town, alive with the flashing signs of noisy cafés. But the men from the *Queen* went straight to the open market which was to be the auction place.

A pile of boxes made a none-too-stable platform on which stood several men, two in the blue-green uniforms of the Survey, one in rough leather and fabric of the town, and one in the black and silver of the Patrol. All the legalities would be strictly observed even if Naxos was sparsely settled frontier.

Nor were the men gathering there all wearing brown Trade tunics. Some were from the town, come to see the fun. Dane tried to check the badges of rivals by the limited light of the portable flares. Yes, there was an Inter-Solar man, and slightly to his left, the triple circle of the Combine.

The A-s and B-s would be put up first—planets newly contacted by Galactic Survey but with a high degree of civilization—perhaps carrying on interplanetary trade within their own systems, planets which the Companies would find worth dealing with. The C-s—worlds with backward cultures— were more of a gamble and would not be so feverishly sought. And the D-s, those with only the most primitive of intelligent life, or perhaps no intelligent life at all—were the chances within the reach of the *Queen*.

"Cofort is here—" He heard Wilcox tell the Captain and caught Jellico's bitter answering exclamation.

Dane looked more closely at the milling crowd. Which one of the men without Company insignia was the legendary prince of Free Traders; the man who had made so many strikes that his luck was fabulous along the star lanes? But he could not guess.

One of the Survey officers came to the edge of the platform and the noise of the crowd died. His cohort held up a box—the box containing the sealed packets of micro-film—each with the co-ordinates and the description of a newly discovered planet.

The A-s went. There were only three and the Combine man snaffled two of them from the Inter-

Solar bidder. But Inter-Solar did much better with the B-s, scooping up both of them. And another Company who specialized in opening up backward worlds plunged on the four C-s. The D-s——

The men of the *Queen* pressed forward, until with a handful of their independent fellows they were right below the platform.

Rip's thumb caught Dane in the lower ribs and his lips shaped the name, "Cofort!"

The famous Free Trader was surprisingly young. He looked more like a tough Patrol Officer than a Trader, and Dane noted that he wore a blaster which fitted so exactly to the curve of his hip that he must never be without it. Otherwise, though rumor credited him with several fortunes, he was little different in outward appearance from the other Free Traders. He made no display of wrist bands, rings, or the single earring the more spectacular of the well-to-do Traders flaunted, and his tunic was as plain and worn as Jellico's.

"Four planets—D class—" the voice of the Survey officer brought Dane's attention back to the business at hand. "Number One—Federation minimum bid—Twenty thousand credits——"

There was a concentrated sigh from the *Queen*'s crew. No use trying for that. With such a high minimum they would be edged out almost before they had begun. To Dane's surprise Cofort did not bid either and it went to a Trader from the rim for fifty thousand.

But at the presentation of planet number two, Cofort came to life and briskly walked away from the rest of the field with a bid of close to a hundred thousand. No one was supposed to know what information was inside each of those packets, but now they began to wonder if Cofort did have an advance tip.

"Planet Three—D class—Federation minimum bid —Fifteen thousand——"

That was more like it! Dane was certain Van Rycke would rise to that. And he did, until Cofort over-topped him with a jump from thirty to fifty thousand in a single offer. Only one chance left. The men from the *Queen* drew together, forming a knot behind Van Rycke as if they were backing the Cargo-Master in a do or die effort.

"Planet Four—D Class—Federation minimum bid fourteen thousand—"

"Sixteen—" Van Rycke's boom tripped over the Survey announcement.

"Twenty—" that was not Cofort, but a dark man they did not know.

"Twenty-five—" Van Rycke was pushing it.

"Thirty—" the other man matching him in haste.

"Thirty-five!" Van Rycke sounded confident as if he had Cofort's resources to draw upon.

"Thirty-six—" the dark trader turned cautious.

"Thirty-eight!" Van Rycke made his last offer.

There was no answer. Dane glancing saw that Cofort was passing over a voucher and collecting his two packets. The dark man shook his head when the Survey man turned to him. They had it!

For an instant the *Queen*'s men could hardly believe in their good luck. Then Kamil let out a whoop and the staid Wilcox could be seen pounding Jellico on the back as Van Rycke stepped up to claim their purchase. They spilled out into the street, piling in and on the scooter with but one thought in mind—to get back to the *Queen* and find out what they had bought.

3   CHARTERED GAMBLE

THEY WERE ALL in the mess cabin again, the only
space in the *Queen* large enough for the crew to
assemble. Tang Ya set a reader on the table while
Captain Jellico slit the packet and brought out the
tiny roll of film it contained. Dane believed afterward that few of them drew a really deep breath until
it was fitted into place and the machine focused on
the wall in lieu of the regular screen.

"Planet—Limbo—only habitable one of three in
a yellow star system—" the impersonal voice of
some bored Survey clerk droned through the cabin.

On the wall of the *Queen* appeared a flat represen-
tation of a three world system with the sun in the
center. Yellow sun—perhaps the planet had the
same climate as Terra! Dane's spirits soared. Maybe
they were in luck—real luck.

"Limbo—" that was Rip wedged beside him.
"Man, oh, man, that's no lucky name—that sure
isn't!"

But Dane could not identify the title. Half the
planets on the trade lanes had outlandish names
didn't they—any a Survey man slapped on them.

"Co-ordinates—" the voice rippled out lines of formulae which Wilcox took down in quick notes. It would be his job to set the course to Limbo.

"Climate—resembling colder section of Terra. Atmosphere—" more code numbers which were Tau's concern. But Dane gathered that it was one in which human beings could live and work.

The image in the screen changed. Now they might be hanging above Limbo, looking at it through their own view ports. And that vision was greeted with at least one exclamation of shocked horror.

For there was no mistaking the cause of those brown-gray patches disfiguring the land masses. It was the leprosy of war—a war so vast and terrible that no Terran could be able to visualize its details.

"A burnt off!" that was Tau, but above his voice rose that of the Captain's.

"It's a filthy trick!"

"Hold it!" Van Rycke's rumble drowned out both outbursts, his big hand shot out to the reader's control button. "Let's have a close up. North a bit, along those burn scars—"

The globe on the screen shot toward them, enlarging so that its limits vanished and they might have been going in for a landing. The awful waste of the long ago war was plain, earth burned and tortured into slag, maybe still even poisonous with radioactive wastes. But the Cargo-Master had not been mistaken, along the horrible scars to the north was a band of strangely tinted green which could only be vegetation. Van Rycke gave a sigh of satisfaction.

"She isn't a total loss—" he pointed out.

"No," retorted Jellico bitterly, "probably shows

just enough life so we can't claim fraud and get back our money.''

"Forerunner ruins?" the suggestion came from Rip, timidly as if he felt he might be laughed down.

Jellico shrugged. "We aren't museum men," he snapped. "And where would we have to go to make a deal with them—off Naxos anyway. And how are we going to lift from here now without cash for the cargo bond?"

He had hammered home every bad point of their present situation. They owned ten-year trading rights to a planet which obviously had no trade— they had paid for those rights with the cash they needed to assemble a cargo. They might not be able to lift from Naxos. They had taken a free Trader's gamble and had lost.

Only the Cargo-Master showed no dejection. He was still studying the picture of Limbo.

"Let's don't go off with only half our jets spitting," he said mildly. "Survey doesn't sell worlds which can't be exploited——"

"Not to the Companies, no," Wilcox commented, "but who's going to listen to a kick from a Free Trader—unless he's Cofort!"

"I still say," Van Rycke continued in the same even tone, "that we ought to explore a little farther——"

"Yes?" Jellico's eyes held a spark of smoldering anger. "You want us to go there and be stranded? She's burnt off—so she's got to be written off our books. You know there's never any life left on a Forerunner planet that was assaulted——"

"Most of them are just bare rock now," Van

Rycke said reasonably. "It looks to me as if Limbo didn't get the full treatment. After all—what do we know about Forerunners—precious little! They were gone centuries, maybe even thousands of years, before we broke into space. They were a great race, ruling whole systems of planets and they went out in a war which left dead worlds and even dead suns swinging in its wake. All right.

"But maybe Limbo was struck in the last years of that war, when their power was on the wane. I've seen the other blasted worlds—Hades and Hel, Sodom, and Satan, and they're nothing but cinders. This Limbo still has vegetation. And because it isn't as badly hit as those others I think we might just have something—"

He is winning his point, Dane told himself— noticing the change of expression on the faces around the table. Maybe it's because we don't want to believe that we've been taken so badly, because we want to hope that we can win even yet. Only Captain Jellico looked stubbornly unconvinced.

"We can't take the chance," he repeated, his lips in an obstinate line. "We can fuel this ship for one trip—*one* trip. If we make it to Limbo and there's no return cargo—well," he slapped his hand on the table, "you know what that will mean—dirt-side for us!"

Steen Wilcox cleared his throat with a sharp rasp which drew their attention. "Any chance of a deal with Survey?" he wanted to know.

Kamil laughed, scorn more than amusement in the sound. "Do the Feds ever give up any cash once they get their fingers on it?" he inquired.

No one answered him until Captain Jellico got to his feet, moving heavily as if some of the resilience had oozed out of his tough body.

"We'll see them in the morning. You willing to try it, Van?"

The Cargo-Master shrugged. "All right, I'll tag along. Not that it'll do us any good."

"Blasted—right off course——"

Dane stood again at the open hatch looking out into a night made almost too bright by Naxos' twin moons. Kamil's words were not directed to him, he was sure. And a moment later that was confirmed by an answer from Rip.

"I don't call luck bad, man, 'til it up and slaps me in the face. Van had an idea—that planet wasn't blasted black. You've seen pictures of Hel and Sodom, haven't you? They're cinders, as Van said. This Limbo, now—it shows green. Did you ever think, Ali, what might happen if we walked onto a world where some of the Forerunners' stuff was lying around?"

"Hm—" the idea Rip presented struck home. "But would trading rights give us ownership of such a find?"

"Van would know—that's part of his job. Why—" for the first time Rip must have sighted Dane at the hatch, "here's Thorson. How about it, Dane? If we found Forerunner material could we claim it legally?"

Dane was forced to admit that he didn't know. But he determined to hunt up the answer in the Cargo-Master's tape library of rules and regulations.

"I don't think that the question has ever come

up," he said dubiously. "Have they ever found usable Forerunner remains—anything except empty ruins? The planets on which their big installations must have been are the burnt off ones——"

"I wonder," Kamil leaned back against the hatch door and looked at the winking lights of the town, "what they were like. All of the strictly human races we have encountered are descended from Terran colonies. And the five non-human ones we know are all as ignorant of the Forerunners as we are. If they left any descendants we haven't contacted them yet. And—" he paused for a long moment before he added, "did you ever think it is just as well we haven't found any of their installations? It's been exactly ten years since the Crater War——"

His words trailed off into a thick silence which had a faint menacing quality Dane could not identify, though he understood what Kamil must be aiming at. Terrans fought, viciously, devastatingly. The Crater War on Mars had been only the tail end of a long struggle between home planet and colonist across the void. The Federation kept an uneasy peace, the men of Trade worked frantically to make that permanent before another and more deadly conflict might wreck the whole Service and perhaps end their own precarious civilization.

What *would* happen if weapons, such as the Forerunners had wielded in their last struggle, or even the knowledge of such weapons, fell into the wrong Terran hands? Would Sol become a dead star circled by burnt off cinder worlds?

"Sure, it might cause trouble if we found weapons," Rip had followed the same argument.

"But they had other things besides arms. And maybe on Limbo——"

Kamil straightened. "Maybe on Limbo they left a treasure house stored with bags of Thork gems and Lamgrim silk—or their equivalent, sure. But I don't think the Captain is in the mood to hunt for it. We're twelve men and one ship—how long do you think it would take us to comb a whole planet? And our scout flitters eat fuel too, remember? How'd you like to be stranded dirtside on some planet like this Naxos— have to turn farmer to get food? You wouldn't care for it."

Dane had to admit inwardly that *he* certainly wouldn't care for that. And if the *Queen* did set down so—locked in some port for the lack of funds to get her off-world again, he wouldn't even have his back pay as a meager stake to tide him over until he could get another ship. The others must be thinking of that also.

Sometime later Dane lay awake on his narrow bunk amazed at how quickly all their hopes had crashed. If Limbo had only proved to be what they first thought—or even if they only had a big enough reserve to go and inspect their purchase— But— suddenly Dane sat up—there had been that other Trader who had bid against Van Rycke at the auction. Could he be persuaded to take Limbo off their hands at a big discount?

But with a burnt off, he wouldn't want it even at half what they had paid Survey. The risk was too great—no one would make a dry-run on such short odds. Only a man with Cofort's backing could take a

38

chance—and Cofort had shown no interest in this particular "bargain."

In the morning it was a glum crew who trailed in and out of the mess cabin. All of them carefully avoided the end of the table where a grim Captain Jellico sat sipping at a cup of Mura's own secret brew which was usually served only at moments of rejoicing. This was no celebration—it must be that the steward believed they needed heartening.

Van Rycke came in, his tunic sealed trimly from his belt to his broad chin, his winged officer's cap perched on his head, ready for a town visit. Jellico grunted and pushed away his cup as he arose to join him. And so daunting was the Captain's scowl that not one of the others dared to wish them good luck on their mission.

Dane climbed down into the cargo hold, studying its empty space and making a few measurements of his own. If they were fortunate enough to get a pay load he wanted to be ready for its stowing. The hold was in two sections—a wide chamber which took in almost a third of the ship and a small cabin sized space above it in which choice or unusual items could be stored.

In addition, on the same level, was the tiny room where was shelved and boxed their "trade goods," small items used to attract the attention of savages or backward civilizations—gadgets, mechanical toys, trinkets of glass, wire, enameled metal. Dane, trying out his memorization of the store catalogue, made the rounds of the cases. He had been taken on two tours of inspection by Van Rycke, but he had not yet lost his sense of wonder at the kinds and quality of the goods, and the display of knowledge and imagination of the Cargo-Master who had assembled this collection. Here were the presents for chieftains and petty kings, the exciters which would bring the people of primitive villages flocking to view such off-world wonders. Of course the supply was strictly limited, but it had been chosen with such care, such insight into humanoid and X-Tee psychology that it must go a long way to win customers for the *Queen*.

Only on Limbo such preparations would be useless. It was not possible that any intelligent life had survived the burn off. If there had been any natives the Survey team would certainly have reported them and that might have raised the value of the planet— even kept it out of the Trade auction until government men had more time to study it.

Dane tried to forget the fiasco of Limbo by applying himself to the study of the ''contact'' goods. Van Rycke had been patient with him on their rounds of this store house, using incidents from his own past to point up the use of each object in the cases or on the protected shelves. Some of the material, Dane gathered, was the handiwork of the crew.

Long drives through space, with the ship locked on its automatic controls, with few duties for her crew, tended to become monotonous. Boredom led to space mania and those who followed the Galactic lanes had early learned that skills of brain and hand were the answer. These could vary widely.

On board the *Queen*, Captain Jellico was a xenobiologist, far past amateur standing. While he could not bring back his specimens alive—save for such "pets" as the blue Hoobat now caged in his cabin—the tri-dee shots he had taken of animal life on unknown worlds had earned him fame among naturalists. Steen Wilcox, whose days were spent wrestling with obtuse mathematics, was laboring to transpose such formulae into musical patterns. And the oddest employ Dane had so far uncovered among his new companions was that of Medic Tau who collected magic, consorting with witch doctors and medicine men of alien primitives, seeking to discover the core of truth lying beneath the mumbojumbo.

Dane picked up a piece of Mura's handiwork, a plasta-crystal ball in which floated, to all examination alive, a rainbow winged insect totally unfamiliar to him. But a shadow gliding in the panel to his left brought him out of his absorption. Sinbad, the *Queen*'s cat, leaped gracefully to the top of a case and sat there, regarding the apprentice. Of all the native Terran animals the one which had most easily followed man into space was the feline.

Cats took to acceleration, to free fall, to all the other discomforts of star flight, with such ease that there were some odd legends growing up about their tribe. One was that Domestica Felinus was not really native to Terra, but had descended from the survivors of an early and forgotten invasion and in the star ships he was only returning to his former golden age.

But Sinbad and those of his species served a definite purpose on board ship and earned their pay. Pests, not only the rats and mice of Terra, but other and odder creatures from alien worlds, came aboard with cargo, sometimes not to be ordinarily detected for weeks, even months after they had set up house-keeping in the hidden corners of the ship. These were Sinbad's concern. When and where he caught them the crew might never learn, but he presented the bodies of the slain to Van Rycke. And, from all accounts, on past voyages some of the bodies had been very weird indeed!

Dane held out his hand and Sinbad sniffed lazily at his fingers and then blinked. He accepted this new human. It was right and proper for Dane to be here. Sinbad stretched and then leaped lightly down from the box to go about the room on regular patrol. He lingered near one bale with such profound sniffing that Dane wondered if he shouldn't open it for the cat's closer inspection. But a distant gong startled them both and Sinbad, one who never overlooked the summons to a meal, flashed out of the room, leaving Dane to follow at a more dignified pace.

Neither the Captain nor the Cargo-Master had returned, and the atmosphere at mess continued to be sober. With two other Free Traders in port any cargoes, too small to tempt Company ships, would be at a premium. But they were all startled when the communication light from the outer hatch clicked on overhead.

Steen Wilcox jumped for the corridor and Dane was only seconds behind him. With Jellico and Van Rycke off ship, Wilcox was the nominal commander of the *Queen,* and Dane the representative of *his* section—on duty until the Cargo-Master returned.

A scooter was drawn up at the foot of the ramp, its

driver sitting behind the controls. But a tall man, thin and burnt brown, was climbing confidently up to the entrance hatch.

He wore a scuffed, hard duty leather tunic and frab-cord breeches, with thigh-high boots of corval skin, the dress of a field man on a pioneer world. On the other hand he did not affect the wide brimmed hat of the men Dane had seen in town. Instead his head was covered with a helmet of Metaplast which had the detachable visor and the bubble ear pockets of a built in short wave receiver—the usual head gear of a Survey man.

"Captain Jellico?" his voice was crisp, authoritative, the voice of a man who was used to giving orders and having them unquestioningly obeyed.

The astrogator shook his head. "Captain's planet-side, sir."

The stranger halted, drumming his fingers on his wide, pocket-walled belt. It was plain he was annoyed at not finding the commander of the *Queen* on board.

"When will he be back?"

"Don't know." Wilcox was not cordial. Apparently he had not taken a fancy to the caller.

"You are open to charter?" was the other's surprising inquiry.

"You'll have to see the Captain—" Wilcox's coolness grew.

The tattoo of fingers on the belt became faster. "All right, I'll see your Captain! Where is he—can you tell me that?"

A second scooter was approaching the *Queen* and

there was no mistaking the bulk of its driver. Van Rycke was returning to the ship. Wilcox had sighted him too.

"You'll know in a minute. Here's our Cargo-Master——"

"So——" the man swung around on the ramp, his lithe body moving with trained speed.

Dane grew intent. This stranger was an intriguing mixture. His dress was that of a pioneer-explorer, his movements those of a trained fighting man. Dane's memory presented him with a picture—the exercise ground at the Pool on a hot summer afternoon. That under swing of the arm—the betraying hunch of the shoulder— This fellow was a force-blade man—and a practiced one! But force-blades—illegal—no civilian was supposed to be familiar with their use.

Van Rycke circled the waiting scooter which had delivered the stranger and came at his usual ponderous pace up the ramp.

"Looking for someone?"

"Is your ship up for charter?" the stranger asked for the second time.

Van Rycke's bushy brows twitched. "Any Trader is always open to a good deal," he answered calmly. "Thorson——" his attention swept past the other's impatience to Dane, "go in to the Green Whirly Bird and ask Captain Jellico to return——"

Dane ran down the ramp and got into Van Rycke's scooter. He glanced back as he put the small vehicle in gear and saw that the stranger was now following the Cargo-Master into the *Queen*.

The Green Whirly Bird was half café, half restaurant and Captain Jellico was seated at a table near the door, talking to the dark man who had bid for Limbo at the auction. But as Dane came into the murky room the other Trader shook his head firmly and got to his feet. The Captain made no move to detain him, only shoved the tankard before him an inch or so to the right, concentrating upon that action as if it were some intricate process he must master.

"Sir——" Dane dared to put a hand on the table to attract attention.

The Captain looked up, and his eyes were bleak and cold. "Yes?"

"There's a man at the *Queen*, sir. He's asking about a charter. Mr. Van Rycke sent me for you——"

"Charter!" The tankard went over on its side, to bump to the floor. Captain Jellico flung a piece of the local metal money on the table and was already on his way to the door, Dane hurrying after.

Jellico took control of the scooter, starting off at a wild pace. But before they had gone the length of the street the Captain slowed and when they drew up before the *Queen* no one could have guessed they were in a hurry.

It was two hours later that the crew assembled once more to hear the news. And the stranger sat with Jellico as the Captain told the crew of their luck.

"This is Dr. Salzar Rich," he made a brief introduction. "He is one of the Federation experts on Forerunner remains. It seems that Limbo isn't such a flame out after all, men. The Doctor informs me that Survey located some quite sizable ruins on the northern hemisphere. He's chartered the *Queen* to transport his expedition there——"

"And," Van Rycke smiled benignly, "this in no way interferes with our own trading rights. We shall have a chance to explore too."

"When do we lift?" Johan Stotz wanted to know.

"When can you be ready, Dr. Rich?" Jellico turned to the archaeologist.

"As soon as you can stow my equipment and men, Captain. I can bring my supplies up right away."

Van Rycke got to his feet. "Thorson." He brought Dane to him with that call. "We'll make ready to load. Send in your material as soon as you wish, Doctor."

4 LIMBO LANDING

DURING THE next few hours Dane learned more in practice about the stowage of cargo than he had ever been taught in theory at the Pool. And, cramped as the crew of the *Queen* were, they also discovered that they must find space for not only Rich but for three assistants as well.

The supplies went into the large cargo hold, most of the work being volunteer labor on the part of Rich's men, since the Doctor hammered home the fact that delicate instruments and perishable goods were included and he had no intention of allowing any of the boxes to be tossed about by the hustlers hired by the Field.

But inside the ship the final stowage of material was, as Van Rycke speedily let him know, solely the problem of the crew. And they could do it without any amateur advice. So Dane and Kosti sweated, swore and tugged, with the Cargo-Master himself not above lending a hand, until all the supplies were in place according to the mechanics of weight for take-off. Then they sealed the hatch for the duration of the flight.

On their way up they discovered Mura in the smaller cargo compartment rigging space hammocks for Rich's assistants. The accommodations were crude but the archaeologist had been warned of that before he had thumbprinted the charter contract—the *Queen* had no extra passenger cabins. And none of the newcomers were grumbling.

Like their leader they were a type new to Dane, giving an impression of tough endurance—a quality which, he supposed, was very necessary in any field man sent out to prospect on strange worlds for the relics of vanished races. One of them wasn't even human—the greentinted skin and hairless head stamped him a Rigellian. But his faintly scaled body, in spite of its odd sinuosity, was clad just like the others. Dane was trying not to stare at him when Mura came up and touched his arm.

"Dr. Rich is in your cabin. You've been moved into the store cubby—along here——"

A little irked by being so high-handedly assigned to new quarters, Dane followed Mura down to the domain, which was the steward's own. There was the galley, the food storage freezers, and, beyond, the hydro garden which was half Mura's concern, half Tau's, as air officer.

"Dr. Rich," Mura explained as they went, "asked to be near his men. He made quite a point of it——"

Dane looked down at the small man. Just why had Mura added that last?

More than any of the crew Mura presented an enigma to Dane. The steward was of Japanese descent—and the apprentice had been familiar from

48

his early training days with the terrifying story of
what had happened to those islands which had once
existed across the sea from his own native country.
Volcanic action, followed by tidal waves, had over-
whelmed a whole nation in two days and a night—so
that Japan had utterly ceased to be—washed from the
maps of Terra.

"Here," Mura reached the end of the corridor and
waved Dane through a half-open panel.

The steward had made no effort to decorate the
walls of his private quarters, and the extreme neat-
ness of the cabin tended to have a bleak effect. But
on a pull-down table rested a globe of plasta-crystal
and what it contained drew Dane's attention.

A Terran butterfly, its jeweled wings spread wide,
hung by some magic in the very center of the orb,
sealed so for all time, and yet giving every appearance of vibrant life.

Mura, noting Dane's absorption, leaned forward
and tapped the top of the globe lightly. In answer to
that touch the wings seemed to quiver, the imprisoned beauty moved a fraction.

Dane drew a deep breath. He had seen the globe in
the store room, he knew that Mura collected the
insect life of a hundred worlds to fashion the balls—
there were two others on board the *Queen*. One a tiny
world, an aquatic one with fronds of weed curling to
provide shelter for a school of gemmed insect-fish
which were stalked by a weird creature two legged,
two armed, but equipped with wing-like fins and a
wicked pronged spear. That was in a place of honor
in Van Rycke's cabin. Then there was the other—a
vista of elfin towers of silver among which flitted

nearly transparent things of pearly luster. That was the Com-Tech's particular treasure.

"One may create such, yes," Mura shrugged. "It is a way of passing time—like many others."

He picked up the globe, rolled it in protecting fiber and stowed it away in a partitioned drawer, cushioned against the take-off of the *Queen*. Then he pulled aside a second panel to show Dane his new quarters.

It was a secondary store room which Mura had stripped and refurnished with a hammock and a foot locker. It was not as comfortable as his old cabin, but on the other hand it was no worse than the quarters he had had on both the Martian and Lunar training ships during his Pool cruises.

They blasted off for Limbo before dawn and were space borne before Dane aroused from an exhausted sleep. He had made his way to the mess hall when the warning sounded again and he clutched the table, swallowing painfully as he endured the vertigo which signalized their snap into Hyperspace. Up in the control compartment Wilcox, the Captain, and Rip would be at their stations, not able to relax until the break-through was assured.

He wouldn't, Dane decided not for the first time since he had entered training for space, be an astrogator for any reward the Federation could dream up. One fractional mistake in calculations—even with two computers taking most of the burden of the formula runoff—would warp your ship into a totally unknown lane, might bring you *inside* a planet instead of the necessary distance off its surface. He had had the theory of the break-through pounded into him, he could go through the motions of setting up a course, but he privately doubted if he would ever have the courage to actually take a ship into Hyperspace and out again.

Frowning at the unoffending wall he was once more listing his own shortcomings when Rip called.

"Man—" the astrogator-apprentice dropped down on a seat with a deep sigh, "well, we're in once more and nothing cracked!"

Dane was honestly surprised. He was no astrogator, it was all right for him to feel some doubts. But that Rip should display relief at having his own particular share of duty behind him for a while was something else.

"What's the matter?" Dane wondered if something *had* threatened to go wrong.

"Nothing, nothing," the other waved a hand. "But we all feel easier after the jump." Rip laughed now. "Man, you think *we* don't sweat it out? We maybe hate it more than you do. What have you got to worry about until we planet again? Nothing——"

Dane bristled. "No? We've only cargo control, supplies, hydro—" he began to enumerate the duties of his section. "What good does a successful breakthrough do when your air goes bad—"

Rip nodded. "All right, none of us are dead weight. Though this trip—" he stopped suddenly and glanced over his shoulder in a way which surprised Dane.

"Did you ever meet an archaeologist before, Dane?"

The cargo-apprentice shook his head. "This is my

first trip out, remember? And we don't get much briefing in history at the Pool—except where it influences Trade——''

Rip lounged back on the bench, but kept his voice trained low, until it was hardly above a murmur.

"I've always been interested in the Forerunners," he began. "Got the tapes of Haverson's 'Voyages' and Kagle's 'Survey' in my gear now. Those are the two most complete studies that have been made so far. I messed with Dr. Rich this morning. And I'll swear he never heard of the Twin Towers!"

Since Dane had never heard of them either, he couldn't quite see what Rip was trying to prove. But, before he could ask any questions, the blankness of his look must have betrayed his ignorance for the other made a quick explanation.

"Up to now the Twin Towers are about the most important Forerunner find Federation Survey has ever made. They're on Corvo—standing right in the center of a silicon desert—two hundred feet high, looking like two big fingers pointing into the sky. And as far as the experts have been able to discover, they're solid clear through—made of some substance which is neither stone nor metal, but which certainly has lasting properties. Rich was able to cover his slip pretty well, but I'm sure he'd not heard of them.''

"But if they're so important," began Dane and then he grasped what the Doctor's ignorance could mean.

"Yes, why doesn't the Doctor know all about the most important find in his field? That presents a problem doesn't it? I wonder if the Captain checked up on him before he took the charter——''

But Dane could answer that. ''His ID was correct, we flashed it through to Patrol Headquarters. They gave us clearance on the expedition or we couldn't have lifted from Naxos——''

Rip conceded that point. Field regulations on any planet in the Federation were strict enough to make at least ninety percent sure that the men who passed them were carrying proper ID-s and clearance. And on the frontier worlds, which might attract poachers or criminals, the Patrol would be twice as vigilant about flight permission.

''Only he didn't know about the Twin Towers,'' the astrogator-apprentice repeated stubbornly.

And Dane was impressed by the argument. It was impossible to spend a voyage on any star ship with another man and not come to know him with an intimacy which was unknown by civilization outside the small dedicated band of those who manned the Galactic fleets. If Rip said that Dr. Rich was not what he seemed, then Rip was speaking the truth as far as he knew it and Dane was willing to back him.

''What about the law regarding Forerunner remains?'' Shannon asked a moment later.

''Not much about it in the records. There've never been any big finds made by a Trader and claimed under Trading rights——''

''So there's nothing we could quote as a precedent if we did find something worthwhile?''

''That can work both ways,'' Dane pointed out. ''Survey released Limbo for Trade auction. If they did that, it seems to me, they've forfeited any Federation claims on the planet. It would make a nice legal tangle——"

"A beautifully complicated case——" Van Rycke rumbled over their heads. "One which half the law sharks of the systems would be eager to see come to trial. It's the sort of thing which would drag on for years, until all parties concerned were either heartily sick of it or safely dead. Which is just why we are traveling with a Federation Free Claim in our strong box."

Dane grinned. He might have known that such an old hand in Trade as his superior officer would not be caught without every angle covered as far as it was humanly possible. A Free Claim to any finds on Limbo!

"For how long?" Rip was still ridden by doubts.

"The usual—a year and a day. I don't think Survey is as impressed by the possibility of unusual finds as our passengers seem to be."

"Do *you* think we'll discover anything there, sir?" Dane struck in.

"I never advance any guesses on what we'll find on any new planet," Van Rycke answered tranquilly. "There are entirely too many booby-traps in our business. If a man gets away with a whole skin, a space-worthy ship, and a reasonable percentage of profit, the Lords of High Space have been good to him. We can't ask for more."

During the days which followed Rich's men kept very much to themselves, using their own supplies and seldom venturing out of their very constrained quarters, nor did they in turn invite visitors. Mura reported that they seemed to spend more of their time either in sleep or engrossed in some complicated gambling game the Rigellian had introduced.

While Dr. Rich messed with the crew of the *Queen*, he dropped in for his meals at hours when there were few in the cabin. And, either by choice or a too well regulated coincidence, those few were generally members of the engineering staff. On the plea of studying the scene of his future operations he had tried to borrow the Survey tape of Limbo, but the times he had been allowed to use it was under the eye of the Cargo-Master. An eye which, Dane was certain, missed nothing, no matter how abstracted Van Rycke might appear to be.

The *Queen* made transition into normal space on schedule within Limbo's system. Two of the other planets who shared this sun were so far away from that core of light and heat that they were frozen, lifeless worlds. But Limbo swung around on its appointed orbit at about the same range as Mars held in their native system. As they approached to come in a "breaking orbit," allowing the friction of the planet's atmosphere to slow the ship to landing speed, the Com-Tech switched on the vision screens throughout the ship. Strapped down on their pads, those not on duty watched the loom of the new world fill the screen.

The ugly brown-gray scars of the burn off faced them first, but as the ship bored in, always at an angle which would coast it along the layers of air gradually, the watchers sighted the fingers of green and traces of small seas or large lakes which proved that Limbo was not wholly dead, blasted though she had been.

Day became night as they passed on, and then day again. If they had been following the strict regulations for landing on a normal "primitive" world they would have tried for a set-down in a desert country, planning to explore by flitter, learning something in secret of the inhabitants before they made open contact. But Limbo would have no intelligent inhabitants—they could use the best possible landing.

Wilcox had brought them through Hyperspace by his reckoning, but it was Jellico who would set them down after choosing his site. And he was maneuvering to place them on the very edge of the burned area with the healthy ground within easy reach.

It was a tricky landing, not the easy one any tyro could make on a cleared Field with a beam to ride in. But the *Queen* had made such landings before and Jellico nursed her down, riding her tail flames until she settled with a jar which was mild under the circumstances.

"Grounded—" the pilot's voice echoed thinly over the com.

Stotz replied from the engine room with the proper answer: "Secure."

"Planet routine—" Jellico's voice gathered volume.

Dane unstrapped and headed for Van Rycke's office to get his orders. But he had hardly reached the door when he bumped into Dr. Rich.

"How soon can you get the supplies moving out?" the archaeologist demanded.

Van Rycke was still unfastening his shock belts. He looked up in surprise.

"You want to unload at once?"

"Certainly. As soon as you unseal hatch-es——"

The Cargo-Master settled his uniform cap on his light hair. "We don't move quite that fast, Doctor. Not on an unknown world."

"There are no savages here. And Survey has certified it fit for human exploration." The Doctor's impatience was fast becoming open irritation. It was as if during their time in space he had so built up his desire to get to work on Limbo that now he begrudged a single wasted moment.

"Brake your jets, Doctor," the Cargo-Master returned tranquilly. "We move at the Captain's orders. And it doesn't pay to take chances—whether Survey has given us an open sky or not." He touched the ship-com board on the wall by his elbow.

"Control here!" Tang's voice came through.

"Cargo-Master to Control—report all clear?"

"Report not ready," was the return. "Sampler still working——"

Dr. Rich slammed his fist against the door panel. "Sampler!" he exploded. "With a Survey report you want to play around with a sampler!"

"We're still alive," was Van Rycke's comment. "In this business there are risks you take and those you don't. We take the proper ones." He lowered himself into his desk chair and Dane leaned against

57

the wall. The indications were that they were not going to be in a rush unloading.

Dr. Rich, reminding Dane of the Captain's caged Hoobat—though, of course, the archaeologist had not reached the point of spitting at them—snarled and went on toward the cabin where his men were waiting.

"Well," Van Rycke leaned back in his seat and flipped a finger at the visa-screen, "we can't call that a pleasant vista——"

In the distance were mountains, a saw-toothed chain of gray-brown rock crowned in some instances with snow. And their foothills were a ragged fringe cut by narrow, crooked valleys, in the mouths of which a pallid, unhealthy vegetation grew. Even in the sunlight the place looked dreary—a background for a nightmare.

"Sampler reports livable conditions——" the disembodied voice from control suddenly proclaimed.

Van Rycke touched the com-call again. "Cargo-Master to Captain, do you wish exploring parties prepared?"

But he had no answer for that as Dr. Rich burst in upon them again. And this time he pushed past Van Rycke to shout into the com-mike:

"Captain Jellico—this is Salzar Rich. I demand that you release my supplies at once, sir, at once!"

His first answer was complete silence. And Dane, awed, questioned within himself whether the Captain was simply so angry that he couldn't reply coherently. One didn't demand that a star ship captain do this or that—even the Patrol had to "request."

"For what reason, Dr. Rich?" To Dane's surprise the voice was quiet, unruffled.

"Reason!" sputtered the man leaning across Van Rycke's desk, "why, so that we may establish our camp before nightfall——"

"Ruins to the west——" Tang's calm announcement cut through Rich's raised voice.

All three of them looked at the visa-screen where the mountains to the north had disappeared, to be replaced by the western vista as the Com-tech swung the detector from one compass point to the next.

Now they were gazing out over the burnt ground, where the unknown weapons of the Forerunners had scored down to rock and then scarred the rock itself with deep grooves filled with a glassy slag which caught and reflected the sun's rays in bright flashes. But beyond this desolation was something else, a tumble of edifices which reached on into the un-devastated circle of vegetation.

The ruins were a blotch of bright color in the general somberness, spilling in violent reds and yellows, strident greens and blues. They were, perhaps, some twenty miles from the *Queen*, and they were spectacular enough to amaze the three in the Cargo-Master's office. Perhaps because Dr. Rich was now treading on familiar ground he was the first to regain speech.

"There——" he jabbed an impatient finger at the screen, "that's where we'll camp!" He whirled back to the mike and spoke into it:

"Captain Jellico—I wish to establish my camp by those ruins. As soon as your Cargo-Master will re-lease our supplies——"

His vehemence appeared to win, for a short time later Van Rycke broke the seals on the cargo hatch, the Doctor impatient beside him, the three other members of his expedition lined up in the corridor behind.

"We will take over now, Van Rycke——"

But the Cargo-Master's arm was up, barring the Doctor's advance.

"No, thank you, Doctor. No load goes out of the *Queen* unless my department oversees the job."

And with that Rich had to be content, though he was fuming as Dane operated the crane swinging out and down the ship's radar controlled crawler. And it was the apprentice who supervised the unloading. The Rigellian climbed up on the crawler, using its manual controls to guide it to the ruins. Once unloaded there it could return by itself, guided by the ship's beam, for a second cargo.

Rich and two of the others rode away on the second trip and Dane was left with the silent fourth member of the expedition to wait for the crawler. The last load was a small, miscellaneous one, mostly the personal baggage of the men.

Over the manifest disapproval of the expedition man the Cargo-apprentice piled the bags up ready for a quick packing. But it was the other who dropped a battered kit bag. It fell heavily, its handle catching on a spur of rock, ripping it open.

With a muffled exclamation the man sprang to stuff back the contents, but he was not quick enough to hide the book which had been wrapped in an undershirt.

That book! Dane's eyes narrowed against the sun.

But he had no time for a second glance at it—the man was already strapping shut the bag. Only Dane was sure he had seen its twin—sitting on Wilcox's flight desk. Why should an archaeologist be carrying an astrogator's computer text?

5 FIRST SCOUT

DUSK ON Limbo had an odd, thick quality as if the shadows were of a tangible dimension. Dane saw to the closing of the outer cargo hatch, leaving the crawler, which had returned empty from its last trip across the barrens, parked on the scorched earth under the fins of the *Queen*. They had taken all the other precautions of a ship on an unknown planet. The ramp had been warped in, the air locks closed. To Limbo at large the *Queen* presented sleek smooth sides which nothing outside of some very modern and highly technical weapons could breach. No star Trader ever took to space except in a ship which could serve as a fort if the need arose.

Intent on his own problem Dane climbed from level to level until he reached Rip's confined quarters on the fringe of control territory. The astrogator-apprentice was huddled on a snap-down seat, a T-camera in his hands.

"I got a whole strip of the ruins," he told Dane excitedly as the other paused in the doorway. "But that Rich— He's a free-rider if I ever saw one. Wonder Sinbad didn't hunt him out with the rest of the cargo gnawers and turn him in as legitimate prey——"

"What's he done now?"

"With the biggest thing yet in Forerunner finds out there," stabbing a finger toward the wall, "he's sitting on it as if it is his own personal property. Told Captain Jellico that he didn't want any of us going over to see things—that 'the encroachment of untrained sightseers too often ruined unusual finds'! Untrained sightseers!" Rip repeated the words deep in his throat, and, for the first time since Dane had known him, he registered real resentment.

"Well," Dane pointed out reasonably, "even with four to help him he can't cover the whole planet. We're going to send out a scouting team after the regular system, aren't we? What's to prevent your running down some class-A ruins of your own? I don't think Rich's found the only remains on the whole planet. And there's nothing in the rules which says we can't explore the ones *we* find."

Rip brightened. "You're blasting with all jets now, man!" He put the T-camera down.

"At least," Kamil's carefully enunciated words cut in from the corridor, "one can never accuse the dear Doctor of neglect of duty. The way he rushed off to the scene of his labors you'd think he expected to find someone there cutting large slices out of the best exhibits. The dear Doctor *is* a bit of a puzzle all around, isn't he?"

Rip voiced his old suspicion. "He didn't know about Twin Towers——"

"And that red-headed assistant of his carries an astrogator's computer text in his kit bag." Dane was very glad to have information of his own to add to the discussion, especially since Kamil was there to hear it. The quiet with which his statement was received was flattering. But as usual Ali provided the first prick.

"How did that amazing fact come to your attention?"

Dane decided to ignore the faint but unpleasant accent on "your."

"He dropped his kit bag, the book rolled out, and he was in a big hurry to get it out of sight again."

Rip reached out to pull open a cupboard. From within he produced a thick book with a water-and-use-proof cover. "You saw one like this?"

Dane shook his head. "His had a red band—like the one on Wilcox's control cabin desk."

Kamil whistled softly and Rip's dark eyes went wide. "But that's a master book!" he protested. "No one but a signed-on astrogator has one of those, and when he signs out of any ship *that* goes into the Captain's safe until his replacement comes on board. There's just one on every ship by Federation law. When a ship is decommissioned the master book for it is destroyed——"

Ali laughed. Don't be so naïve, my friend. How do you suppose poachers and smugglers operate? Do they comb their computations out of the air? It wouldn't surprise me if there was a brisk black market trade in computer texts, long since supposed to be burnt."

But Rip still shook his head. "They wouldn't have the new data—that's added on each planet as we check in. Why do you suppose Wilcox goes to the

Field control office with our volume every time we set down on another world? That book is sent straight to the local Survey office and is processed to add the latest dope. And you couldn't present anything but a legit text—they'd spot it in a minute!''

"Listen, my innocent child," drawled Kamil, "for every law the Federation produces in their idealist vacuum there is some bright boy—or boys—working day and night to break it. I'm not telling you how they work it, but I'm willing to wager all my cut of this particular venture, that it's being done. If Thorson saw a red badge text book in that fellow's possession, then it's being done right here and now—on Limbo.''

Rip got to his feet. "We should tell Steen——"

"Tell him what? That Thorson saw a book which looked like a text fall out of that digger's personal baggage? You didn't pick it up, did you, Thorson, or examine it closely?''

Dane was forced to admit that he had not. And his deflation began. What proof had he that the man from the expedition possessed a forbidden master text? And Steen Wilcox, of all people, was the last man on the ship to approach with a story founded on anything but concrete evidence. Unless Dane had the volume in question in his hand and ready to show, he would have little chance of being believed.

"So you see," Kamil turned back to Rip, "we'll have to have much better proof in our hot little hands before we go bursting in on our elders in the guise of intrepid Fed Agents or Boy Patrolmen.''

Rip sat down again, as convinced of the reasonableness of that argument as Dane was. "But," he pounced upon the bit of encouragement in that crushing speech, "you say 'we'll have to have'—Then you *do* believe that there's something wrong with the Doctor!"

Kamil shrugged. "To my mind he's as crooked as a Red Desert dust dancer, but that's just my own private and confidential opinion, and I'm keeping it behind my nice white teeth until I can really impress the powers that be. In the meantime, we're going to be busy on our own. We're drawing for flitter assignments within the hour."

The small flitters carried by the *Queen* for exploration work held with comfort a two-man crew—with crowding, three. Both of the planes had been carefully checked by the engineering section that afternoon while Dane had been busied with unloading the expedition supplies. And there was no doubt that the next morning would see the first of the scouting parties out on duty.

There were no lights to break the somber dark of Limbo's night. And then men of the *Queen* lost interest in the uniformly black visa-screens which kept them in touch with the outside. It was after the evening meal that they drew for membership on the flitter teams. As usual the threefold organization of the ship determined the drawing; one man of the engineers, one of the control deck, and one of Van Rycke's elastic department being grouped together.

Dane wanted to be teamed with Rip if he had open choice. He thought rather bitterly afterward that maybe it was because of that strong desire that he was served just the opposite. For, when he drew his slip, he discovered that his running mates were

Kamil and Tang. A re-arrangement by the Captain left him in the end with the Medic Tau in place of the Com-Tech who—for some purpose of his own— Jellico decreed must remain with the *Queen*.

More than a little disgusted at such luck he moved back into his old cabin. Curiosity led him to a minute search of the limited storage space, in a faint hope that perhaps he could find some forgotten possession of the enigmatic doctor. Now if this were a Tel-Video melodrama he, as the intrepid young hero, would discover the secret plans of— But that thought led him to remember Kamil's common sense appraisal of their position with regard to unsubstantial suspicions.

And then he was thinking of Kamil, trying to analyze why he so much disliked the engineer-apprentice. Ali's spectacular good looks and poise were part of it. Dane was not yet past the time when he felt awkward and ill at ease on social occasions—he still bumped into objects—just as on the parade ground at the Pool the instructors had used him as an example of how not to execute any maneuver. And when he looked in the small mirror above him on the cabin wall, his eyes did not observe any outward charm. No, physically Kamil was all Dane was not.

In addition the Cargo-apprentice suspected that the other had a quickness of wit which also left him at the post. He, himself, was more of the bulldog type, slow and sure. While Kamil leaped ahead with grasshopper bounds. The right sort of bounds, too. That was the worst of it, Dane had argued himself into a rueful amusement. You wouldn't dislike the engineer so much if he were wrong just once in a while. But so far Ali Kamil had proved to be disgustingly right.

Well, even though the Psycho fitted you to a ship and its crew—you couldn't be expected to like everyone on board. Machines had their limitations. He could rub along with most people, that was one good and useful thing he had learned at the Pool.

Deciding there was no profit in seeking trouble before it sneaked up to use a blaster on one, Dane went to sleep. And in the early dawn of the next day he was eager for the adventure of a scout.

Captain Jellico respected the wishes of Dr. Rich to the extent of not setting any course toward the ruins. But on the other hand he made his instructions plain to the crews of both small ships. Any signs of new Forerunner finds were to be reported directly to him—and not on the broadcaster beam of the flitters—a broadcast which could be picked up by those in Rich's camp.

Dane strapped on his helmet with its short wave installation, fastened about his waist an explorer's belt with its coil of tough, though slender rope, its beam light, and compact envelope of tools. Though they did not expect to be long from the *Queen*, into the underseat storage place on the flitter went concentrated supplies, a small medical kit, and their full canteens, as well as a packet of trade "contact" goods. Not that they would have any use for that in Dane's estimation.

Ali took the controls of the tiny ship while Dane and Tau shared a cramped seat behind him. The engineer-apprentice pushed a button on the board and the curved windbreak slid up and over, enclosing them. They lifted smoothly from the side of the *Queen*, to level off at the height of her nose, swinging north for the route Jellico and Van Rycke had charted them.

The sun was up now, striking fire from the slag rivers on the burnt land, bringing to life the sickly green of the distant vegetation which formed tattered edging on the foothill valleys. Dane triggered the recording camera as they winged straight for the northern range of mountains.

As they crossed into the sparse clusters of brush, Ali automatically lost altitude and slowed pace, giving them a chance for a searching examination of what lay below. But Dane could see no signs of life, insect or animal, and no winged things shared the morning air with them.

They followed the first narrow valley to its end, combing it for anything of interest. Then Ali turned to the right, zooming up over a saw-edged ridge of naked black rock, to seek the next cut of fertile soil. Again only scant brush and scattered clumps of grass were to be seen.

But the third valley they explored was more promising. Down its center coursed a small stream and the vegetation was not only thicker but a darker, more normal shade of green. Dane and Tau sighted the first find almost together and their voices formed a duet:

"Down!"

"There!"

Ali had swept over the spot, but now he cut speed and circled back while the other two plastered themselves against the transparent windbreak, trying to sight that strange break in the natural spread below.

There it was! And Dane's excitement grew as he knew that he had been right at his first guess. That pocket-sized, regularly fenced space was a field under cultivation. But what a field! The enclosure, with its wall of pebbles and brush, couldn't have been more than four feet square.

Growing in straight rows was a small plant with yellow, fern-like leaves, a plant which trembled and shook as if beaten by a breeze—when none of the neighboring bushes moved at all.

Ali circled the spot twice and then coasted down the valley toward the devastated plain. They passed three more separate fields and then a larger space where the valley widened out and accommodated three or four together. All of them were fenced and bore evidence of careful tending. But there were no pathways, no buildings, no traces of who or what had planted and would harvest those crops.

"Of course," Tau broke the perplexed silence first, "we may have here a flora civilization instead of a fauna—"

"If you mean those carrot-topped things down there built the walls and then planted themselves in rows—" began Ali, but Dane could think of an answer for that. As a Cargo man he had been too firmly indoctrinated with the need for keeping an open mind when dealing with X-Tee races to refuse any suggestion without investigation.

"This could be the nursery—the adults could have planted seeds——"

Ali's answer to that was a snort of derision. But

Dane did not allow himself to show irritation. "Can we set down? We ought to have a closer look at this—"

"Well away from the fields," he added that caution a moment later.

"Listen, you bead merchant," Ali snapped, "I'm not green and rocket shaken——"

He'd deserved that, Dane decided honestly. This was *his* first field trip—Ali was his superior in experience. No more backseat flitter control from now on. He shut his mouth tight as Ali spiraled them down toward a space of bare rock well away from both the stream and the fields it watered.

Tau made contact with the *Queen*, reporting their discovery, and orders came that they were to explore the valley discreetly, seeking any other signs of intelligent life.

The Medic studied the cliffs near which they had landed. "Caves—" he suggested.

But, though they walked for some distance beside those towering reaches of bare black rock, there were no hollows nor crevices deep enough to shelter a creature even the size of Sinbad."

"They may have hidden from the flitter," remarked Ali. "And they could be watching us from cover right now."

Dane turned in a full circle, scanning with wary eyes not only the cliff walls, but the clumps of brush and the taller stands of coarse grass.

"They must be small," he muttered half to himself. "Those fields are so limited in area."

"Plants," Tau returned to his own pet theory. But Dane was not yet ready to agree.

"We've contacted eight X-Tee races so far," he said slowly. "The Sliths are reptilian, the Arvas remotely feline, the Fifftocs brachiopod. Of the rest, three are chemically different from us, and two—the Kanddoyds and the Mimsis—are insects. But a vegetable intelligence——"

"Is perfectly possible," Tau finished for him.

They made a careful inspection of the nearest field. The quivering plants stood about two feet high, their lacy foliage in constant flickering motion. They had been carefully spaced apart by the planters and between them the ground was bare of any weed or encroaching spear of grass. The Terrans could see no fruit or seeds on the slender stems, though, as they stooped for a closer look they became aware of a strong spicy scent.

Ali sniffed: "Clove—cinnamon? Somebody's herb garden?"

"Why herbs and nothing else?" Dane squatted on his heels. What was the most puzzling to him was the absence of paths. These miniature gardens were carefully tended, yet there were no roads connecting them, no indication that the invisible farmers approached them on foot. On foot—! Was that a clue, a winged race? He mentioned that.

"Sure," Ali used his usual deflating tactics, "a bunch of bats and they only come out at night. That's why there's no greeting committee on hand——"

Nocturnal? It was entirely possible, Dane thought. That meant that the Terrans must establish a contact station and man it through the dark hours. But if the farmers went about their work in utter darkness they were going to be difficult to watch. All the men from the *Queen* could do was to set up the station and look after it for the rest of the day, hoping it was only that their strange presence was what had terrified the inhabitants of the valley into hiding.

But, though Tau and Dane concealed themselves thoroughly in the shadow of tall rocks while Ali lifted the flitter to the top of the cliff well out of sight, the hours crawled on and there was nothing to be seen but the shivering spicy plants and their wild cousins along the stream.

Whatever life did exist on Limbo must be limited both in numbers and varieties. Along with samples of water and vegetation, Tau captured an earth colored insect bearing a close resemblance to a Terran beetle, imprisoning it in a small tube for transportation to the *Queen*, and a future study. And another insect with pale, wide wings dipped toward the water an hour later. But animals, birds, reptiles, all were missing.

"Anything which survived the burn-off," Tau half whispered, "must have been far down the scale——"

"But the fields," protested Dane. He had been trying to figure out a possible lure for the mysterious Limbians, if and when they appeared. Having no idea as to their nature, he was faced with a real problem in contact. What if their eyesight differed—the brightly colored trifles designed to attract the usual primitive races would then be worthless. And if their auditory sense was not within human range the music boxes which had been used to such

73

excellent advantage in establishing friendly relations with the Kanddoyds could not be brought out. He was inclined to dwell on the scent of the field plants. Their spiciness, which was so strong that it was thick to notoriously dull human nostrils, was the only distinctive attribute he had to follow. A contact baited with scent—spicy scent—might just work. He asked Tau a question:

"Those plants are aromatic. Do you have anything like that scent in your medical stores? I've some perfumed soap from Garatole in my trade kit, but that's pretty strong——"

Tau smiled. "The problem of bait, eh? Yes, scent might just bring them in. But, look here, I'd try Mura's stores instead of the medical ones. Get some pinches of his spices——"

Dane leaned back against the rock. Now why hadn't he thought of that! Flavors used in cooking—sure, Mura might have some substance in the galley which would attract a people who raised the lacy leaved herbs. But he'd have to go back to the *Queen* to see——

"I'd say," the Medic continued, "that we're not going to make contact today. It's my guess they're nocturnal and we should rig a contact point on that theory. Let's go——"

As the senior officer of the scouting party, Tau had the right to make such a decision. And Dane, eager to start his own preparations for contact, was ready to agree. They waved the flitter down and reported back to the *Queen*, getting orders to return.

They were received in the Captain's office and the

Cargo-Master and Jellico heard them out, allowing Dane to state his suggestion concerning the use of spice to draw the Limbians from hiding. When he had spilled it out in eager enthusiasm, the Captain turned to Van Rycke.

"What about it, Van? Ever use spices in a contact?"

The Cargo-Master shrugged. "You can make contact with anything which will attract an X-Tee, Captain. I'd say this is worth a try—along with the rest of the usual stuff."

Jellico picked up his com-mike. "Frank," he said into the phone, "come up here and bring samples of all your spices—anything with a strong, pleasant odor."

Two hours later Dane studied his handiwork with what he hoped was the necessary critical appraisal. He had selected a broad rock mid-way between two of the small fields. On the stone he had arranged materials from a basic trade kit. There was a selection of jewelry, small toys, metallic objects, which would easily catch the eye, then a music box arranged to be triggered into tune if handled. And last of all three plastic bowls, each covered with a fine gauze through which came the aroma of mixed spices.

Behind a bush was concealed the contact visa-view which would record any approach to that rock for the benefit of those in the flitter on the cliffs above—where he, Tau, and Kamil would spend the night on watch.

He was still a trifle amazed that he had been

allowed to take over this presentation—but he had discovered that the creed of the *Queen* was just—the idea was his, he was to carry it out—the success or failure would depend on him. And he was uncertain within as he climbed into the flitter for the rise to the cliff tops.

6   SINISTER VALLEY

AGAIN DANE was conscious of the thick quality of the Limbian night. Since the planet possessed no satellite, there was nothing to break the dark but those cold pin points which marked the stars. Even the visa-screen they had set up below could hardly pierce the gloom, though it was equipped with a tri-strength delve-ray.

Tau stretched and shifted in his seat, inadvertently nudging Dane. Although they were wearing double-lined winter outer tunics and the temperature of the closed flitter was supposedly akin to the interior of the *Queen*, an insidious chill caught at them. They had divided the night into watches, the two off duty at the tiny receiving screen trying to nap. But Dane found rest beyond him. He stared out at the dark which folded about them like a smothering curtain.

He did not know what time it was that he saw the first flash—a red sword of light striking up into the sky in the west. At his exclamation Ali on duty at the screen glanced up and Tau stirred into wakefulness.

"Over there!" They might not be able to follow his pointing finger but by now they needed no such guide. The flashes of light were multiplied—then they were gone—leaving the night darker than ever.

It was Ali who spoke first: "Blaster fire!" His fingers were already busy on the keys, flashing a message to the *Queen*.

For an instant Dane felt a prick of panic and then he realized that the disturbance was far westward of the *Queen*. The ship had *not* been attacked in their absence. Ali reported the evidences of distant battle. From the ship the flares had not been sighted and the men there knew nothing of any trouble. Nor had they seen, across the barrens, any disturbance at the ruins where Rich was encamped.

"Do we stick here?" Ali asked a last question. And the reply came promptly that they should—unless forced to withdraw. It was more than ever necessary to discover the nature of any native Limbian life.

But the screen which connected them with the valley below remained obstinately dark. There was the rock, the trade goods, and nothing else.

They kept two watches now, one for the screen and the other westward. But no more flares split the night. If a battle had been in progress it was now over.

By Dane's reckoning it was close to dawn and it was his trick at the screen when the first hint of change came. The movement on the plate before him was so slight that at first he thought he had been mistaken. But a bush to the right of the rock below provided a dark background for something so weird he could not believe he was seeing aright. Luck alone, and reflex action, pressed his finger down on the button of the recorder at the right moment.

For the thing was not only unsubstantial, it was also fast, moving at a speed which blurred its already wispy outline. Dane had seen something, he was sure of that. But what it had been, even its general form, he could not have sworn to.

With both Ali and Tau breathing down the back of his neck, Dane hung over the screen, alert to the slightest movement on its surface. But, though dawn was upon them, and the light was growing better all the time, they could see nothing now but leaves fluttered by the wind. Whatever had passed that way had had no interest in the trade display. They would have to depend upon the film from the recorder to discover what it was.

Limbo's sun began the upward climb. The rime of nightborn frost which had gathered on the stones of the heights was lapped away. But the valley remained deserted, Dane's visitor did not return.

The other flitter arrived with a fresh crew to take over the post. Rip walked over to speak to the yawning crew of the first.

"Any luck?" he wanted to know.

"Got something with the recorder—I hope," Dane replied, but he was feeling more apologetic than triumphant. That faint shadowy thing might not be the owner of the fields—just some passing animal.

"Captain says for you to take a look-see down west before you check in," Rip added to Tau. "Use your own judgment, but don't run into anything serious if you can help it."

The Medic nodded. Ali was at the controls and

they took to the air, leaving the relieving crew of the
other flitter to take over their watch. Below them
spread the now familiar pattern of small, narrow
valleys, two or three showing squares of fields. But
though Ali buzzed at a low altitude over these, there
was no life but vegetation below. The Terran flitter
was perhaps five miles on to the west before it came
down over a scene of horror.

Smoke still curled sluggishly from smoldering
brush and the black burns of high voltage blaster fire
crossed and re-crossed the ground, cutting noisome
paths through greenery and searing soil and rock.

But it was not that which attracted their attention.
It was the *things*, three of them, huddled together in a
rock pocket as if they had tried to make a last stand
there against a weapon they did not understand. The
contorted, badly burned bodies had little recogniz-
able form now, but the three in the flitter knew that
they had once been living creatures.

Ali went for a short run above the valley floor.
There was no sign of any life. He maneuvered for a
landing close to that pocket. But it wasn't until they
had left the flitter and started to cross a rocky outcrop
that they came upon the fourth victim.

He—or it—had been singed by the flame, but not
killed at once. Enough will to live had remained to
send the pitiful wreckage crawling into a narrow
crevice where it must have clung until death
loosened its hold and allowed it to tumble slackly
into sight again.

Tau went down on one knee beside the twisted
body. But Dane, his nostrils filled with a sickening
stench which was not all born of the smoldering

green stuff, took only one quick look before he closed his eyes and fought a masterly engagement with his churning stomach.

That hadn't been a man! It resembled nothing he had ever seen or heard described. It—it wasn't real—it couldn't be! He gained a minor victory, opened his eyes, and forced himself to look again.

Even allowing for the injuries which had killed it, the creature was bizarre to the point of nightmare. Its body consisted of two globes, one half as large as the other. There was no discernible head at all. From the larger globe protruded two pair of very thin, four jointed limbs which must have been highly flexible. From the small globe another pair which separated at the second joint into limber tentacles, each of which ended in a cluster of hair-fine appendages. The globes were joined by a wasp's slenderness of waist. As far as Dane could see, and he couldn't bring himself to the close examination which absorbed Tau, there were no features at all—no eyes, ears, or mouth.

But the oddest sight of all were the globes which formed the body. They were a grayish-white, but semi-transparent. And through the surface one could sight reddish structural supports which must have served the creature as bones, as well as organs Dane had no wish to explore.

"Great space!" Ali exploded. "You can look right through them!"

He was exaggerating—but not so much. The Limbians—if this were a Limbian—were far more tenuous than any creature the Terrans had found before. And Dane was sure that the record film would show that it was a thing such as this which had passed the contact point in the other valley.

Ali stepped around the body to examine the scars left by the blast which had driven the creature into the crevice. He touched a finger gingerly to a blackened smear on the rock and then held it close to his nose.

"Blaster right enough."

"Do you think Rich—?"

Ali gazed down the valley. Like all the others they had yet sighted it ran from the towering mountains to the blasted plain, and they could not be too far from the ruins where the archaeologists had gone to earth.

"But—why?" Dane asked a second question before his first had been answered.

Had the globe things attacked Rich and his men? Somehow Dane could not accept that. To his mind the limp body Tau was working over was pitifully defenseless. It held not the slightest hint of menace.

"That's the big question." Ali tramped on, past the hollow where lay those other dreadfully contorted bodies, down to the edge of the stream, which this valley, as did all the cultivated ones, cradled in its center, the fields strung out along it.

Plain to read here was the mark of the invader. No feet had left that pair of wide ruts crushed deep into the soft ground of the fields. Dane stopped short.

"Crawler! But our crawlers——"

"Are just where they should be, parked under the *Queen* or in their storage compartments," Ali finished for him. "And since Rich couldn't have

82

brought one here in a kit bag, we must believe that Limbo is not as barren of life as Survey certified it to be.'' He stood at the edge of the stream and then squatted to study a patch of drying mud. ''Track's odd though——''

Although his opinion had not been asked, Dane joined the Engineer-apprentice. The tread marks had left a pattern, clear as print, for about four inches. He was familiar with the operation of crawlers as they pertained to his own duties. He could even, if the need arose, make minor repairs on one. But he couldn't have identified any difference in vehicles from their tread patterns. There he was willing to accept Ali's superior learning.

Kamil's next move was a complete mystery to Dane. Still on his knees he began measuring the distance between the two furrows, using a small rule from his belt tool kit for a gauge. At last Dane dared to ask a question:

''What's wrong?''

For a moment he thought that Ali wasn't going to answer. Then the other sat back on his heels, wiped dust from the rule, and looked up.

''A standard crawler's a four-two-eight,'' he stated didactically. ''A scooter is a three-seven-eight. A flamer's carriage runs five-seven-twelve.''

The actual figures meant very little to Dane, but he knew their significance. Within the Federation machinery was now completely standardized. It had to be so that repairs from one world to the next would be simplified. Ali had recited the measurements of the three types of ground vehicles in common use on the majority of Federation planets. Though, by rights, a flamer was a war machine, used only by the military or Patrol forces, except on pioneer worlds where its wide heat beam could be turned against rank forest or jungle growth.

"And this isn't any of those," Dane guessed.

"Right. It's three-two-four—but it's heavy, too. Or else it was transporting close to an overload. You don't get ruts like these from a scooter or crawler traveling light." He was an engineer, he should know, Dane conceded.

"Then what was it?"

Ali shrugged. "Something not standard—low, narrow, or it couldn't snake through here, and able to carry a good load. But nothing on our books is like it."

It was Dane's turn to study the cliffs about them. "Only one way it could go—up—or down——"

Ali got to his feet. "I'll go down," he glanced over at the busy Tau engrossed in his grisly task, "nobody's going to drag him away from there until he learns all he can." He shuddered, perhaps in exaggeration, perhaps in earnest. "I have a feeling that it isn't wise to stay here too long. Any scout will have to be a quick one——"

Dane turned upstream. "I'll go up," he said firmly, it was not Ali's place to give orders, they were equal in rank. He started off, walking between the tracks without looking back.

He was concentrating so on his determination to prove that he could think properly for himself that he made a fatal slip, inexcusable in any Trade-explorer. Though he continued to wear his helmet, along with all the other field equipment, he totally forgot to set his personal com-unit on alert, and so went blindly off into the unknown with no contact with either of the others.

But at the moment he was far more intent on those tracks which lured him on, up a gradually narrowing valley toward the mountain walls. The climbing sun struck across his path, out there were pools of purple shadow where the cliffs walled off its rays.

The trail left by the crawler ran as straight as the general contour of the ground allowed. Two of the lacy winged flying things they had glimpsed in the other valley skimmed close to the surface of the stream and then took off high into the chill air.

Now the greenery was sparser. He had not passed a field for some time. And underfoot the surface of the valley was inclining up in a gentle slope. The walls curved, so that Dane walked more warily, having no desire to round a projection and meet a blaster user face to face.

He was certain in his own mind that Dr. Rich had something to do with this. But where did this crawler come from? Had the Doctor been on Limbo before? Or had he broken into some cache of Survey supplies? But there was Ali's certainty that the vehicle was not orthodox.

The trail ended abruptly and in such a manner as to stop Dane short, staring in unbelief. For those ruts led straight to a solid, blank wall of rock, vanishing beneath it as if the machine which had made them had been driven straight through!

There is always, Dane hastily reminded himself, some logical explanation for the impossible. And not Video ones about "force walls" and such either. If those tracks went into the rock, it was an illusion—or an opening—and it was up to him to discover which.

His boots crunched on sand and gravel until he was in touching distance of the barrier. It was then that he became aware of something else, a vibration. It was very silent there in the cramped pocket which was the end of the valley, no wind blew, no leaves rustled. And yet there was something unquiet in the air, a stirring just at the far edge of his sensitiveness to sound and movement.

On impulse he set the palms of his hands against the stone of the cliff. And he felt it instantly, running up his arms into his body until his flesh and bones were only a recorder for that monstrous beat-beat-beat—relayed to him through the stuff of Limbo itself. Yet, when he passed his fingers searchingly over the rough stone, studied each inch of it intently, he could see no break in its surface, no sign of a door, no reason for that heavy thump, thump which shook his nerves. The vibration was unpleasant, almost menacing. He snatched his hands away, suddenly afraid of being trapped in that dull rhythm. But now he was sure that Limbo was not what it seemed—a lifeless, dead world.

For the first time he remembered that he should have maintained contact with the others, and hurriedly turned the key on his com-unit. Instantly Tau's voice rang thinly in his ears.

"Calling Ali— Calling Thorson—come in—come in!" There was an urgency in the Medic's voice which brought Dane away from the wall, set him on the back trail even as he replied:

"Thorson here. Am at end of valley. Wish to report—"

But the other cut into that impatiently. "Return to flitter! Ali, Thorson, return to Flitter!"

"Thorson returning." Dane started at the best pace he could muster down the valley. But as he trotted, slipping and sliding on the loose stones and gravel, Tau's voice continued to call Ali. And from the engineer-apprentice there came no answer at all.

Breathing hard, Dane reached the place where they had left the Medic. As he came into sight Tau waved him to the side of the flitter.

"Where's Ali?" "Where's Kamil?" Their demands came together and they stared at each other.

Dane answered first. "He said he was going downstream—to follow the crawler tracks we found. I went upstream——"

"Then it must have been he who—" Tau was frowning. He turned on his heel and studied the valley leading to the plains. The presence of water had encouraged a thicker growth of brush there and it presented a wall except for where the stream cut a passage.

"But what happened?" Dane wanted to know.

"I got a call on com—it was cut off almost immediately—"

"Not mine, I was off circuit," returned Dane before he thought. It was only then that he realized what he had done. No one on field duty goes off circuit out on scout, that was a rule even a First Circler in the Pool had by heart. And he had done it the first time he was on duty! He could feel the heat spreading up into his cheeks. But he offered no explanations nor excuses. The fault was his and he would have to stand up to the consequences.

"Ali must be in trouble." Tau made no other comment as he climbed in behind the controls of the flitter, a very quiet Dane followed him.

They arose jerkily, with none of the smooth perfection Ali's piloting had supplied. But once in the air Tau pointed the nose of the flitter down valley, cutting speed to just enough to keep them airborne. They watched the ground below. But there was nothing to see but the marks of blaster fire and beyond undisturbed green broken by bare patches of gravel and jutting rock.

They could also sight the crawler tracks and Dane related the information he had. Tau's countenance was sober.

"If we don't find Ali, we must report to the *Queen*——"

That was only common sense, Dane knew, but he dreaded having to admit his own negligence. And perhaps his act was worse than just carelessness in not using the com-unit, perhaps he should have insisted on their sticking together, deserted though the valley appeared to be.

"We're up against something nasty here," Tau continued. "Whoever used those blasters was outside the law——"

The Federation law dealing with X-Tees was severe, as Dane well knew. Parts of the code, stripped of the legal verbiage, had to be memorized at the Pool. You could defend yourself against the attack of aliens, but on no provocation, except in defense of his life, could a Trader use a blaster or other weapon against an X-Tee. Even sleep rays were frowned upon, though most Traders packed them when going into unknown territory among primitive tribes.

The men of the *Queen* had landed unarmed on Limbo, and they would continue unarmed until such a time as the situation was so grave that either their lives or the ship was in danger. But in this valley a blaster had been used in the wanton indulgence of someone's sadistic hatred for the globe creatures.

"They weren't attacking—those globe things, I mean?"

Tau's brown face was grim as he shook his head. "They had no weapons at all. I'd say from the evidence that they were attacked without warning, just mown down. Maybe for the fun of it!"

And that projected such a picture of horror that Tau, conditioned by life under the Trade Creed, stopped short.

Below them the valley began to widen out, cutting in a fan shape into the plain. There was no sign of Ali anywhere on that fan. He had vanished as if he had stepped through the cliff wall. The cliff! Dane remembering the end of the crawler trail, pressed against the windshield to inspect those walls. But there were no tracks ending before them.

The flitter lost altitude as Tau concentrated on landing. "We must report to the *Queen*," he said as he set them down. Not leaving his seat he reached for the long-range beam mike.

7   SHIP OUT OF SPACE

TAU'S FINGERS clicked the call key of the far-range caster when that sound was drowned out by a wail, both weirdly familiar and strangely menacing. Here on the edge of the burnt-off land there was no soughing of the wind, nothing to break the eternal silence of the blasted country. But this tearing over head brought both of the Terrans to their feet. Tau, out of his greater experience, identified it first.

"A ship!"

Dane was no hundred flight man, but something in that shrieking crescendo splitting the sky above them argued that if a ship were coming in, all was not well with it. He caught at Tau's arm.

"What's the matter?"

The Medic's face paled beneath the dark space tan. He bit hard on his lower lip. And the eyes still fastened on the arch of sky were haunted. When he answered he had to scream to be heard over the rumble.

"She's coming in too fast—not on a braking orbit!"

And now they could see as well as hear—a dark

shape in the morning sky, a shape which tore across that same sky to be gone in an instant to a landing somewhere among those jagged peaks which were the mountains of Limbo's northern continent.

The sound was gone. It was broodingly quiet. Tau shook his head slowly.

"She must have crashed. She couldn't have come out of that one in time."

"What was she?" puzzled Dane. The passage of that shadow had been so quick that he had not been conscious of any identifying outline.

"Too small for a liner, thank the Lord of Far Space. Or at least—I hope it was no liner——"

For a passenger ship to crash would be utter horror. Dane could understand that.

"A freighter maybe," Tau sat down and his hand went out to the click keys. "She must have been out of control when she entered atmosphere." He began to relay this last information on to the *Queen*.

They did not have to wait long for an answer. They were to remain where they were until the second flitter joined them carrying Tau's full medical kit. This flyer would then head out into the mountains in an attempt to locate the scene of the crash, so if there were any survivors the men from the *Queen* could render aid. A smaller party would stay and try to trace Kamil.

It was only a matter of minutes before the other flitter did appear. Kosti and Mura dropped from it almost before it hit dirt and Tau hurried across to change place. The flyer whirled up into the sun of mid-morning and cut a straight course toward the rock teeth of the range, following the line of flight Dane and Tau had seen that shadow travel.

"Did you see her from the *Queen?*" Dane demanded of the other two.

Mura shook his head. "See her, no, hear her, yes. She was out of control!"

Kosti's broad face wrinkled in concern. "She must have hit hard. A bad smash—no one living, perhaps. I once saw a smack landing like that on Juno—very bad—all dead. That ship—she must have been out of control before they started down. She was not even fighting the fall—she came in like a thing already dead."

Mura whislted softly. "Plague ship, maybe—"

Dane shivered. Plague ships were the terrifying ghosts of the space lanes. Wandering derelicts, free roving tombs holding the bodies of the crews who on some uncharted world had contracted some new and virulent disease, dying alone in the reaches of the heavens—perhaps by stern choice—before they could bring their infection to inhabited worlds. The solar system guards had the unenviable task of rounding up such drifting threats of death and sending them into cleansing suns or giving them some other final end. But here, beyond the frontiers of civilization, a derelict could drift for years, even centuries, before some freak of chance brought it into the gravitational pull of a planet and so crash it on an unwary world.

But the men of the *Queen* knew the score, there would be no rash exploration of the ship if they did locate it. And its smash-up might have been a thousand miles away, well out of the range of the flitter.

Tau was there—and of all men a Medic was the last to take any chances with a plague.

"Ali—he has disappeared?" Kosti brought them back to the business at hand.

Dane, not overlooking his own carelessness, reported in detail what had happened in the valley. To his relief neither of the newcomers made any comment on his part in the affair, but centered their attention on the task at hand. Mura was the first to suggest a plan of action.

"Let Kosti take up the flitter and cruise above us. Then you and I shall search the ground. There may be some trace left which you could not easily sight from the air."

So it was arranged. The flitter, cut to its lowest cruising speed, circled slowly around, never venturing too far ahead. While Dane and Mura on foot, having to swing bush knives in places against the thick mat of vegetation, made their way into the sinister valley. They found the place where the track of the crawler came from the rock of the burnt-off land to bite into the soft soil of the healthy area.

Mura turned there and stared back, over the plain. They could not sight from this point the blotch of brightly colored ruins. But they were certain that the crawler had come out of the blasted area, to be driven with intelligent purpose toward the mountains—until it vanished into the solid rock of a cliff wall!

"Dr. Rich's party—?" Dane aired his suspicions.

"Perhaps—perhaps not," was Mura's ambiguous reply. "Did you not say that Ali thought this machine was not of the usual type?"

"But—" Dane gaped, "you can't mean that the Forerunners survived—here!"

Mura laughed. "They say that all things are possible in space, do they not? But no, I do not think that those ancient rulers of the lanes have here left their sons to greet us. Only they may have left other things—which are now being put to use. I would like to know more about those ruins—a great deal more."

Perhaps the guess Rip had made days earlier—that on some planet might lie, waiting to be discovered, possessions of the legendary Forerunners—was close to the truth. Had such a cache been discovered by parties unknown here on Limbo? But with that marched the grim warning voiced by Ali that Forerunner material in Terran hands might be a threat to all of them.

Slowly they combed the mouth of the valley, reassured by the flitter cruising above. Dane broke open his field rations, chewing as he went, on a cube of rubbery, tasteless stuff which was supposed to provide his lank young body with all it needed in the way of balanced nourishment—and yet which was so savorless and far removed from real food.

He hacked at a mass of prickly shrubs and stumbled through the clutch of longer branches to come into a pocket-sized clearing entirely ringed with thorn-studded greenery. Under foot was a thick mat of decaying leaves through which not even the spears of grass could grow.

Dane stopped short. The brown muck of the mat had been disturbed. He was conscious of an unwholesome reek of decay which came from scuffed patches where a green slime had been recently uncovered.

He went down on his hands and knees, circling that plowed up patch. He was no tracker, but even to his inexperienced eyes this had been the site of a scuffle. And since the slime was still uncrusted, that event had taken place not too long ago. Dane surveyed the brush which walled in the tiny area. It was just the place for an ambush. If Kamil had come through—over there——

Taking care not to disturb the churned muck, Dane made his way to the opposite side of the clearing. He was right! The cut of a bush knife showed where a branch had been lopped away. Someone, armed with regulation Terran field equipment, had come through here.

Come through here—to find someone, or something, waiting for him!

The globe creatures? Or those who had used the strange crawler and burnt the globes in the valley?

But Dane was certain that he had discovered where Ali had been surprised—not only surprised but overpowered by a superior force. Overpowered—to be taken where? He subjected the walling shrubs to a careful scrutiny. But in no other place did he see any suggestion of disturbance or break. It was almost as if the hunter, having made certain of his prey, had vanished into thin air, transporting the prisoner with him.

Dane was startled by a crashing in the brush. His sleep ray-rod was out as he spun around. But it was Mura's pleasant brown face which was framed in a circle of torn leaves. At Dane's wave he came into

95

the clearing. It was not necessary to point out the signs of battle—he had already noted them.

"They jumped him here," Dane was convinced.

"But who or what are 'they'?" was Mura's counter. And seconds later he added the unanswerable question, "And how did they leave?"

"The tracks of the crawler went right through the wall of the cliff——"

Mura edged out on the carpet of muck. "No indications of any trap door here," he observed, gravely, as if he *had* expected to find something of the sort. "There remains——" he jerked a thumb into the air where the purr of the flitter grew louder as Kosti circled back toward them.

"But we would have heard—have seen——" protested Dane, all the time wondering if they would have. He had been at the other end of the valley when Tau had caught that interrupted cry for help. And from this point the place where the Medic had been at that moment was hidden by at least two miles of broken ground.

"Something smaller than one of our flitters," Mura was thinking aloud. "It could be done. One thing we may be sure of—they have collected Kamil and we must find out who they are and where they are before we can get him back!"

He plowed away through the brush and Dane followed him out on a bare strip of ground from which they could signal to the flitter.

"Found him?" Kosti called as he brought the machine down.

"Found where someone scooped him up." Mura went to the keyboard of the caster.

Dane turned for a last look up that sinister valley. But all at once his attention was drawn from the valley and its cliffs to a new phenomenon in evidence on a higher level. He had not noticed that the sun had disappeared while they had been making their search of the brush. But now clouds were gathering—and not only clouds.

The naked, snow touched peaks of the range, which had been so sharp set against the pallid sky of Limbo when the ship out of space had swept over them, were gone! It was as if that milky, faded sky had fallen as a curtain to blot them out. Where the peaks had been swirled fog—fog so thick that it erased half the horizon as a painter might draw a blotting brush across an unsuccessful landscape. Dane had never seen anything like it. And it was moving so fast, visibly cutting off miles of territory in the few moments he had watched it. To be lost in that——!

"Look!" he ran to the flitter and jogged Mura's arm, pointing to the fast disappearing mountains. "Look at that!"

Kosti spit out an oath in the slurred speech of Venus. Mura simply obeyed orders and looked. Another huge section to the north was swallowed up as he did so. And now they noted another thing. From the tops of the valley cliffs curls of grayish, yellow vapor were rising, to cling and render misty the outlines of the rocks. Whether this was all part of the same they did not know, but the three Terrans insensibly drew closer together, chilled as much by what they saw, as the cold apparent with the going of the sun.

They were shaken out of their absorption by the click of the caster summoning them back to the ship. The change on the mountains had been noted on the *Queen* and both the flitter searching for the wreck and their own were ordered to report in at once.

There was further change in the atmosphere, a speeding up of the mists— The swirls above the valley walls combined, formed banks and began to drop, cutting visibility.

Kosti watched them anxiously. "We'll have to swing out—away from the valleys. That stuff is moving too fast. We *can* ride the beam in, but I'd rather not unless I have to——"

But, by the time they were airborne, the mist was down to the level of the valley floor and was puffing out in threatening tendrils onto the rough terrain of the burnt-off land. The mountains had vanished and the foot-hills were being fast swallowed up. It was uncanny, terrifying in a way, this wiping away of solid earth, the substitution of a dirty, rolling mist which swirled and spun within its mass until one suspicioned movement there, alien, menacing movement.

Kosti set the controls to full speed, but they had covered little more than a mile of the return journey before he was forced to throttle down. For the mist was not only spilling out of the valleys, it was also curling up from the land under them, each thread of haze spinning to join and thicken with others.

It was true that they were in no danger of being lost. The thin reed of sound humming in their ears provided a guide to bring the flitter back to the parent ship. But they were none the easier knowing that as they coasted above a curdling sea of mist.

The stuff rose about them forming viscid bubbles on the windbreak. Only the constant hum of the radar beam linked them with reality.

"Hope our boys made it down from the mountains before the worst of this hit," Kosti broke the strained silence.

"If they didn't," Mura replied, "they will have to land until it clears."

Kosti throttled down once more as the radar hum sharpened. "No use crashing into the old lady——"

Within the blanket of mist all sense of direction, of distance was lost. They might have been up ten thousand feet, or skimming but one above the broken surface of the rock plain. Kosti hunched over the controls, his usually good-humored face pinched, his eyes moving from the mist to the dials before him and back again.

They sighted the ship—a dark shadow looming through the veil. With masterly precision Kosti brought the flitter down until it jarred against the ground. But he was in no hurry to climb out. Instead he wiped his face with the back of his hand. Maura leaned forward and patted the big man's shoulder.

"That was a good job!"

Kosti grinned. "It had to be!"

They crawled out of the flitter and on impulse, linked hands as they started for the dim pillar which was the *Queen*. The contact of palm against palm was not only insurance and reassurance, but it was also security of a type Dane felt he needed—and guessed that his companions wanted also. The menacing, alien mist pressed in upon them. Its damp congealed greasily on their helmets, dripped from them as they moved.

But ten paces took them to the welcome arch of the ramp and they went up, to stand a moment later in the pleasant light and warmth of the entrance hatch. Jasper Weeks teetered back and forth there, his pallid little face expressing worry.

"Oh—you—" was his unflattering greeting.

Kosti laughed. "Who did you expect, little man—a Sensor dragon breathing fire? Sure, it's us, and we're glad to be back——"

"Something wrong?" Mura interrupted.

Weeks stepped to the outer opening of the hatch once more. "The other flitter—we haven't heard from them for an hour. Captain ordered them back as soon as he saw the fog closing in. Survey tape says these fogs sometimes last a couple of days—but they aren't usual this time of the year."

Kosti whistled and Mura leaned back against the wall, unbuckling his helmet.

"Several days." Dane thought of that. To be lost out in that soup for days! You'd just have to stay grounded and hope for the best. But an emergency landing in the mountains under such conditions—! Now he could understand why Weeks fidgeted at the hatch. Their own journey over the unobstructed plain was, under the circumstances, as a stroll in a Terran park, compared to the difficulties those on the other flitter might be forced to face.

They went up to make their report to the Captain. But all through it he sat with at least half of his attention given to the com where Tang Ya sat before the master visascreen, his hand ready for the key of the caster or to tend the rider beam which might guide the missing flyer in. Somewhere out in the mystery which was now Limbo was not only Ali, but Rip, Tau and Steen Wilcox—a good section of their crew.

"There it is again!" Tang's forehead creased, his hands pulled the phones from close contact with his ears. As he did so the rest heard the clamor which had jolted him. Not unlike the drone of the rider beam—it scaled up to a screech which was real pain.

It continued steadily for a space and as Dane listened to it he became conscious of something else—a muffled rhythm deep within that drone—a rhythm he had known before—when he laid his hands upon the wall of the sinister valley. This disturbance was akin to the vibration in the distant rock!

Then, as suddenly as it had begun, the sound was gone. Tang put on his earphones once more and listened for a signal—either from the missing flitter or from Ali's personal com-unit.

"What is that?" Mura asked.

Captain Jellico shrugged. "Your guess is as good as ours. It may be a signal of some sort—been cutting in at regular intervals all day."

"So we must admit—" that was Van Rycke looming in the door of the control cabin, "that we are not alone on Limbo. In fact there is much more to Limbo than meets the casual eye."

Dane voiced his own suspicion. "Those archaeologists—" he began, but the Captain favored him with a sharp pointed stare that stopped him almost in mid-word.

"We have no idea what is at the root of this," Jellico said coldly. "You men get some food and rest——"

Dane, smarting from his abrupt dismissal, trailed Mura and Kosti down to the mess cabin. As they passed the Captain's private quarters they could hear the wild shrieks of the Hoobat. That thing sounded, Dane thought, just the way he felt. And even warm food, bearing no resemblance to the iron rations he had eaten earlier, did little to raise the general curtain of gloom.

But the meal had an excellent effect on Kosti's spirits. "That Rip," he announced to the table at large, "he's got a lot of sense. And Mr. Wilcox, he knows what he's doing. They're all snug somewhere and'll stay holed up until this stuff clears. Nobody'll come out in this——"

Was Kosti right there, Dane wondered. Suppose there were those on Limbo who knew the tricks of the climate, who were familiar enough with such fogs to be able to navigate through them—use them as a cover—? That signal they had heard blatting out of the com—could it be a beam to guide some expedition creeping through the mist? An expedition heading toward the unsuspecting *Queen!*

8   FOG BOUND

THOSE OF THE *Queen*'s men who had no definite
duties engaging them elsewhere drifted to the hatch
which gave upon the gray wool of the new Limbian
landscape. They would have liked to hole up close to
the control section and Tang's com, but the presence
of the Captain there was a dampener. It was better to
hunker down at the top of the ramp, look out into the
mist, and strain one's ears for the motor purr of a
flitter which did not arrive.

"They're smart," observed Kosti for the twen-
tieth time. "They won't risk their necks plowing
through this muck. But Ali—that's different. He was
snatched before this started."

"You think it is poachers?" ventured Weeks.

His big partner considered the point. "Poachers?
Yeah—but on this Limbo what have they got to
poach—tell me that? We aren't pulling in a cargo of
sveek furs, nor arlun crystals—leastways I haven't
seen any of those lying around waiting to be picked
up. What about those dead things back in the valley,
Thorson," he turned to Dane, "did they look as if
they had anything worth poaching?"

"They weren't armed—or even clothed—as far as we could tell," Dane replied a bit absently. "And their fields grew spicy stuff I never saw before——"

"Drugs—could it be drugs now?" inquired Weeks.

"A new kind then—Tau didn't recognize the leaves." Dane's head was up as he faced out into the mist. He was almost sure—there—there it was again! "Listen," he caught at Kosti, dragged the big man out on the ramp.

"Hear anything now?" he demanded a moment later.

There was sound in the fog, a fog which was now three parts night, through which the signal light on the nose of the *Queen* could not cut. The regular beat of a true running motor was magnified by some trick of the mist until it seemed that a whole fleet of small flyers was bearing down upon the space ship from all points of the compass.

Dane whirled and brought his hand down on the lever which controlled the lights along the ramp. Even swirled in the fog as they were, some faint gleam might break through to offer a landing mark for the flitter. Weeks had disappeared. Dane could hear the clatter of his space boots on the ladder within as he sped with the news. But before the wiper could have reached control a new marker blazed into view, the full powered searchlight from the nose, a beacon which could not be blanketed out, no matter how its rays were diffused.

And in that same instant a dark object swept by, so close that Dane leaped back, certain it was going to graze the ramp. The beat of the motor was loud, then it thinned, to grow into a roar once more as the shadow appeared for a second time, circling closer to the ground.

It landed with an audible smacking grind which suggested that the fog spoiled distance judgment. And to the foot of the ramp came three figures which continued to be muffled shapes until they were nearly at the hatch.

"Man—oh, man!" Rip's rich voice came to the ears of the watchers as he halted to pat the side of the ship. "It's good to see the old girl again—Lordy, it's good!"

"How did you make it back through this?" Dane asked.

"We had to," the astrogator-apprentice told him simply. "There was no place back in the ranges to set down. Those mountains are straight up and down—or they look that way. We got on the beam—except when— Say, what's the cause of the interference? We were thrown off twice by it. Couldn't cut it out——"

Steen Wilcox and Tau followed him at a slower pace. The Medic moved wearily, his emergency kit in his hand. And Wilcox had only a grunt for the reception party, pushing past them to climb to control. But Rip lingered to ask another question.

"Ali——"

Dane retold the story of what they had discovered in the valley clearing.

"But how—?" was Rip's second puzzled question.

"We don't know. Unless they went straight up. And it wasn't space enough to hold a flitter. But look how those crawler tracks ran straight into the cliff. Rip, there's something queer about Limbo——''

''How far was that valley from the ruins?'' the astrogator-apprentice's voice lost much of its warmth, it was quieter, with a new crispness.

''We were nearer to those than to the *Queen*. But the fog hit us on the way back and we didn't see them—if we did pass over the location.''

''And you couldn't raise Ali on the com-unit after that one interrupted signal?''

''Tang's been trying. And we kept open all the time we were out.''

''They might have stripped that off him at once,'' Rip conceded. ''It would be a wise move for them. He could give us a fix otherwise——''

''But could we get a fix on a com-unit? On one which no one was using—'' Dane began to see a thin chance. ''That is if its power was still working?''

''I don't know. But the range would be pretty limited. We could ask Tang—'' Rip was already on his way up the ladder to where the com-tech was on duty.

Dane glanced at his watch, making a swift calculation squaring ship time with hours measured on Limbo. It was night. Suppose Tang was able to pick up a call from Ali's com-unit—they could not trace it now.

They did not find the com-tech alone. All the officers of the *Queen* were there and again Tang was holding the earphones well away from his head so that they could hear the discordance which beat out from some hidden point in the fog-bound world.

Wilcox spoke as the two younger men came in.

"That's it! Cut right across the rider beam. I got two fixes on it. But," he shrugged, "with the atmospherics what they are and this soup covering everything, how accurate those are is a big question. It comes from the mountains——"

"Not just some form of static?" Captain Jellico appealed to Tang.

"Decidedly not! I don't think it's a signal—though it may be a rider beam. More like a big installation——"

"What kind of installation would produce a broadcast such as that?" Van Rycke wanted to know.

Tang put the earphones down on the snap desk at his elbow. "A good sized one—about as big as the HG computer on Terra!"

There was a moment of startled silence. An installation with the same force as HG on this deserted world! They had to have time to assimilate that. But, Dane noted, not one of them questioned Tang's statement.

"What is it doing here?" Van Rycke's voice held a note of real wonder. "What *could* it be used for——?"

"It might be well," Tang warned, "to know who is running it. Remember, Kamil has been picked up. They probably know a lot about us while we're still in the dark——"

"Poachers——" that was Jellico but he advanced the suggestion as if he didn't really believe in it himself.

"With something as big as an HG com under their control? Maybe——" but Van Rycke was plainly dubious. "Anyway we can't get out and look around until the fog clears———"

The ramp was drawn in, the ship put under regular routine once more. But Dane wondered how many of the crew were able to sleep. He hadn't expected to, until the fatigue produced from the adventures of the past twenty-four hours of duty pushed him under and he spun from one dream to another, always pursuing Ali through crooked valleys and finally between the towering banks of the HG computer, unable to catch the speeding engineer-apprentice.

His watch registered nine the next morning when he approached the hatch open once more on Limbo. But it might have been the depths of night—save the gray of the mist was three or four shades lighter than it had been when he had seen it last. To his eyes however it was as thick as in the hour when they had returned to the ship.

Rip stood halfway down the ramp, wiping his hand on his thigh as he lifted it from the dripping guide rope where the moisture condensed in large oily drops. He raised a worried face to Dane as the other edged along the slippery surface to join him.

"It doesn't seem to be clearing any," Dane stated the obvious.

"Tang thinks he got a fix—a fix on Ali's unit!" Shannon burst out. He reached once more for the guide rope and faced west, staring out into those cottony swirls hungrily as if by will alone he could force the stuff away from his line of vision.

"From where—north?"

"No, west!"

From the west where the ruins lay—where Rich's

party were encamped! Then they were right, Rich had something to do with Limbo's mystery.

"That interference was cut out sometime early this morning," Rip continued. "Conditions must have been better for about ten minutes. Tang won't swear to it, but he's sure himself that he caught the buzz of a live helmet com."

"Pretty far—the ruins," Dane made the one objection. But he was as certain as Rip that if the com-tech mentioned it at all, it was because he had been nine-tenths sure he was right. Tang was not given to wild guesses.

"What are we going to do about it?" the cargo-apprentice added.

Rip twisted his big hands about the rope. "What can we do?" he wanted to know helplessly. "We can't just go off and hope to come up against the ruins. If they had a caster on it would be different——"

"What about that? Aren't they supposed to keep in touch with the ship? Couldn't a flitter get to them riding in on their caster beam?" Dane asked.

"It could —if there were a beam," Rip returned. "They went off the air when the fog came in. Tang has been calling them at ten minute intervals all night—had the emergency frequency in use so they'd be sure and answer. Only they haven't!"

And, without any caster beam to guide it, no flitter could pierce this murk and be sure of landing at the ruins. Yet a com-unit had registered there—perhaps Ali's—and that only a short time ago.

"I've been out there," Rip pointed to the ground they could not see from the ramp. "If I hadn't had a line fastened I'd been lost before I got four feet away——''

Dane could believe that. But he knew the restlessness which must be needling Rip now. To be kept prisoner here just when they had their first clue as to where Kamil might be——! It was maddening in a way. He edged down the slippery ramp, found the cord Rip had left looped there, and took an end firmly in hand, venturing out into the gray cloud.

The mist condensed in droplets on his tunic, trickled down his face, left an odd metallic taint on his lips. He walked on, taking one cautious step at a time, using the rope to keep him oriented.

A dark object loomed out of the gray and he neared it warily, only to recognize it with an embarrassed laugh as one of the crawlers—the one which had made the journey back and forth to deliver Rich's material to his chosen camp site.

Back and forth——

Dane's hand closed on the tread. What if——? They couldn't be sure—they could only hope——

He used the cord to haul himself back to the ramp, the need for haste making him stumble. If what he hoped was true—then they had the answer to their problem. They could find the camp, make a surprise descent upon the archaeologist, a descent which the other might not be prepared to meet.

There was the ramp and Rip waiting. The astrogator-apprentice must have guessed from Dane's expression that he had discovered something, but he asked no questions, only fell in behind as the other hurried into the ship.

''Where's Van Rycke—Captain Jellico?''

"Captain's asleep—Tau made him take a rest," Rip answerered. "Van Rycke is in his cabin, I think."

So Dane made his way to his own superior's office. If only what he hoped *was* true! It would be a stroke of luck—the best luck they had had since that auction had brought them this headache which was Limbo.

The cargo-master was stretched out on his bunk, his hands behind his head. Dane hesitated in the doorway but Van Rycke's blue eyes were not closed and they did roll in his direction. He asked a question first:

"Have you used the crawler in the past two days, sir?"

"To my knowledge no one has—why?"

"Then it was only used for one purpose here," Dane's excitement grew, "and that was to carry Dr. Rich's supplies to his camp——"

Van Rycke sat up. Not only sat up, but reached for his boots and pulled them on his feet.

"And you think that the fix has been left on that camp. It might just be, son, it might just be." He was tugging on his tunic now.

Rip caught on. "A guide all ready to go!" he exulted.

"We hope," Van Rycke applied a cautious warning.

It was the cargo-master who led the way out of the *Queen* once more, back to the parked crawler. The low slung cargo shifter was standing just as Dane had left it in the shelter of the *Queen*'s fins, its blunt nose pointing forward, out of the enclosure of the fins, to make a quarter turn to the west! The auto-fix was still on the camp. Dane took a running jump for the slow moving vehicle and brought it to a stop. But it was on a line which would take it, fog or no fog, straight to the camp where it had carried supplies two days before. And it would provide an unerring guide for men roped to it. They had a chance now to locate Ali.

The cargo-master made no comment but started toward the *Queen*, the others following. Dane glanced over his shoulder at the crawler.

"If we had one of those portable flamers—" he muttered and Rip caught him up on that.

"A sonic screamer would be more to the point!"

Dane was startled. A flamer could be used as a threat or a tool with which to force one's way into a fortification. It need not be a weapon. But a sonic screamer—there was no protection against the unseen waves which could literally tear a man apart. If Rip wanted a screamer he must fear real trouble. Since the *Queen* was a law abiding ship and carried neither fitting the point must remain purely academic.

Van Rycke climbed to control. And as he rapped at the Captain's private cabin they could hear the screaming of the Hoobat. Jellico opened the panel, his face wearing a weary frown. Before he greeted the cargo-master he slapped the cage of the blue creature, setting it to oscillating crazily, but the shaking up did nothing to discourage the throat splitting squalls.

The cargo-master watched the frenzied Hoobat. "How long has Queex been acting that way, Captain?"

Jellico gave the caged captive a baneful glare and then stepped into the corridor away from the din.

"Most of the night. The thing's gone mad, I think." He shut the panel and the shrieks were muffled. "I can't see what sets it off like that."

"Its hearing range goes into the super-sonic, doesn't it?" Van Rycke persisted.

"Four points. But what—" the Captain bit off that "what" and his eyes narrowed. "That blasted interference! Do you suppose that's sonic?"

"Could be. Does Queez howl when it cuts out?"

"We can see—" Jellico made as if to return to his cabin but Van Rycke caught his arm.

"Something more important on the launching cradle now, Captain."

"Such as what?"

"We've found a guide to take us to Rich's camp." Van Rycke explained about the crawler. Jellico leaned against the wall of the corridor, his face impassive. Van Rycke might have been reciting the table of cargo stowing.

"Could just work," was his only comment when the cargo-master concluded. But he did not appear in any hurry to put it to the proof.

Once more the crew assembled by order in the mess room—without Tang who stayed by the com. When Jellico came in he was holding a small silver rod, fastened to a chain locked on his belt.

"We've discovered," he began without preliminaries, "that the supply crawler is still on auto-beam to Rich's camp. It can act as a guide——"

He was answered by a murmur which separated into individual demands to know when they could start. But these died as Jellico hammered the rod on the table top for their attention.

"Lots—" he said.

Mura had them ready, slips of white straw he dropped into a bowl and stirred about with his finger.

"Tang has to stay with the com," Jellico reminded them. "That leaves ten of us—the five with short straws go———"

The steward passed around, holding the bowl above eye level of the seated men. Each, Dane noticed, palmed his choice, not even looking at it. When all had one they opened their hands together displaying their luck.

Short straw! Dane felt a thrill—was it of pleasure or apprehension— He looked around to see who would be his companions on the trip. Rip—Rip's straw was also short! And so was the one between Kosti's grimed fingers. Steen Wilcox showed the next, and the last was Mura's.

Wilcox would be in command—that was good. Dane had every confidence in the taciturn astrogator. And it was odd how luck had ruled. In a way, those whom fate had chosen were the most expendable of the crew. Should disaster strike, the *Queen* could safely lift from Limbo. Dane tried not to think of that.

Jellico grunted when he found himself ruled out of the expedition. He got to his feet and crossed to the wall on the right. There he applied the rod, unsealing some concealed panel. There was a grating sound as if some catch had not been activated for a long time. Then a rack was revealed—a rack of hand blasters! And below them holster belts swung on pegs,

114

full refills, glinting evilly in the light. The arsenal of the *Queen*, which could only be opened when the Captain deemed the situation highly serious.

One by one Jellico lifted out blasters, passing each in turn to Stotz who inspected it closely, flipping the charge slot open and shut before putting it down on the table. Five blasters, five belts complete with recharges. It appeared that Jellico expected war.

The Captain closed the panel and locked it with that master control rod which by Federation law could not leave his person day or night. Now he returned to the table, facing the five who had been chosen. He gestured to the arms. By training they knew how to use blasters, but a Trader might not have to carry one more than once in a lifetime among the stars.

"They're all yours, boys," he said. And he needed to add nothing to impress upon them just how bad he considered their task to be.

9   BLIND HUNT

ONCE MORE Dane put on his field equipment, making a fervid promise to himself as he adjusted his helmet that this time his com would be on—all the time. No one had said anything to him about his slip-up in the valley. He had thought that his carelessness would condemn him to the side-lines. Yet here he was being given a second chance, merely because he had been lucky in the drawing. And no one had challenged his right to go out. So it was up to him to prove that their confidence was not misplaced.

Since the fog was as heavy as ever there was no day or night outside. They ate a hot and nourishing meal before they tramped into a gloom which their watches told them was mid-afternoon.

With the weight of the blaster resting unfamiliarly against his thigh, Dane followed Rip as Shannon tagged Wilcox's heels down the ramp. Kosti and Mura were already busy at the crawler.

There was room for one man, two if they crowded, on the flat surface of the small vehicle. But, since the platform had no sides and there was nothing to cling to in order to keep from sliding from its fog-slick surface on the rough terrain, the party was content to be infantry, attaching themselves to the guide by lengths of rope.

Kosti triggered the starter and the crawler ground forward, its treads crushing gravel and bits of porous stone. The pace was that of a walk and none of them had any difficulty keeping up.

Dane looked back. Already the *Queen* had vanished. Only a radiance high in the mist marked the searchlight which under ordinary conditions could be seen for miles. It was then that he realized what it would mean to lose touch with the crawler, and his hand tugged the rope which tied them together, testing its safety.

Luckily the ground was fairly even and only once did they have to slip and scramble over one of the rivers of slag. The man who had piloted the crawler across the waste on its first trip to the ruins had chosen the best path he could find.

But they became aware now of another peculiarity of the fog—the noises. Whether those were the sounds they made, flung back and magnified, or some other natural change, they could not tell. But several times they paused, Kosti snapping off the crawler, and listened, sure that they were surrounded by another party moving confidently through the murk, that they were about to be the focus of an attack. But when they so halted the sounds ceased, and it was only when they plodded on once more that the sensation of being dogged by unseen travelers grew strong again. After those two stops, by mutual and unspoken consent, they ignored the noises and pushed on, seeing each other as shadows, the ground under their boots visible only for inches.

The moisture which trickled down their helmets and clothing was an added discomfort. It had, at least to Dane's sensitive senses, an unpleasant smell and it left the skin feeling slimy and unclean. He tried wiping his face vigorously, only to discover that such motion apparently smeared it deeper.

Nothing interfered with the steady advance of the crawler. Though the men who followed it could no longer see the ship, nor sight the ruins for which they were bound, the machine's electronic memory guided them unerringly. They were about three quarters of the way across the waste when they heard a new noise—not raised as an echo of their own passing.

Someone or something running!

And yet that thudding was not the pound of space boots, the rhythm was oddly different—as if the creature who passed had more than two feet, Dane thought.

He faced into the gloom, trying to gauge the quarter from which that sound came. But in the mist the compass points were lost. It could have been speeding toward them or away. Then his guide rope tautened and pulled him on.

"What was that?" the voice was muffled, but it was unmistakably Rip's.

"Your guess is as good as mine." Dane could no longer hear that pattering. Had it been one of the globe things?

A dark object rose out of the fog and then Dane was startled by a shout. His boots rasped from gravel and sand to smoother flooring. He was standing on a square of pavement and that shadow to the left was a jagged wall of ancient ruin. They had crossed the waste!

"Thorson! Dane——!"

Rip's summons was imperative and Dane hurried to answer it. Kosti must have stopped the crawler for his rope did not tug him forward. Then he came upon the astrogator-apprentice bending over a sprawled form.

It was Rip's own chief, Wilcox, who had taken that misstep and now lay partly in the crevice which had clamped knee high on his leg.

In the end it took all four of them to pry the astrogator loose. And it was at least a half hour before he sat on the crawler, nursing his leg where the tough material of the age-old building had punched a jagged hole through the calf of his high boot and drawn blood. They applied first aid, but from now on Wilcox would have to ride.

They closed in a tight escort about the crawler as it moved on. Wilcox sat with a drawn blaster balanced on his good knee. The scraps of ruin became whole walls, sections of oddly shaped structures. And yet they saw nothing which had any signs of a Terran camp.

Here among the relics of an older and alien life Dane felt again that sensation of being spied upon, that just beyond vision limited by the fog lurked something else, something to which these drifting mists were no sight barrier. The treads of the crawler no longer crackled on rock and an eerie silence wrapped them about. The smooth walls ran with dank water, it gathered in puddles here and there. But the liquid was tainted, noisome, with an evil metallic smell clinging about it.

They came into a region where the buildings appeared to be untouched, with roofs and walls still guarding pitch dark interiors. The last thing Dane wanted to do was to explore any of those fetid openings.

But the crawler was not pausing anywhere along the street, instead crunching on over buckled strips of pavement. Perhaps the walls banked off some of the fog, for Dane now found it possible to see not only the forms but the faces of his companions. And all of them, he saw, had a tendency to look over their shoulders, and to stare into the interior of every structure they passed.

It was Rip who made the first find. He had taken out his hand torch and was using it at pavement level. Now he centered that ring of light on a dark splotch which marked a wall a little above ground surface. He tugged a signal to halt and went down on one knee beside his find as Dane joined him.

The cargo-apprentice found the other smelling that splotch, sniffing as if he were some hound on a muddled trail. But to Dane it was only a dark blotch.

"What is it?"

Rip's light swept from the stain on the wall to move over the pavement as if in search. Then it centered on a brownish wad. But though Rip inspected that with care he avoided touching it.

"Crax seed——"

Dane had been stooping. Now, in instant reaction to those words, he straightened. "Sure?"

"Smell it."

But Dane made no move to follow that suggestion. The less one meddled with crax seed the safer one was.

Rip got to his feet and hurried on to the crawler. "There's a cud of crax seed been spit out here. Fairly fresh—maybe this morning——"

"Told you—poachers!" Kosti broke in.

"So—" Wilcox gripped his blaster more firmly. Crax seed was one of the Galaxy wide outlawed drugs. Those unwise enough to chew it had—for a period of time—an abnormal reaction speed, a heightened intellect, a superman control. What occurred to them later was not pretty at all. But to come up against a crax chewer was to face an opponent who at his peak was twice as wily, twice as fast, twice as strong as yourself. And it was not an assignment to be lightly undertaken.

Save for that betraying wad of crax seed, in spite of the search they now made in the vicinity, they could find no other indication that any life but themselves had walked this way since the forgotten war had blasted the city. If Dr. Rich had begun any archaeological excavations, the site of the investigation was still to be found.

Wilcox set the crawler on the lowest speed and started on. Nor was he the only one to travel with his blaster ready. All four of the rest took the same precaution.

"I wonder—" Dane had been surveying the broken line of roofs. "The fog," he added to Rip, "doesn't it appear to be thinner ahead?"

"It's been thinning out ever since we made that

last halt. Good thing, too. Just look at that, man!''

What in a deeper murk, might have been a death trap gaped before them, a vast crevice slicing the pavement, opening a pit large enough to swallow both the crawler and the men escorting it. But the machine was prepared for that. Ponderously it altered course eastward, pulling up over a mound of rubble while Wilcox had to reholster his blaster and cling with both hands to keep his seat. The machine reached the top of the mound and began to crawl down the opposite side, a crawl which became a slide as the earth gave way beneath its weight.

Surely that rumble was enough to rouse any of Rich's men. But though those from the *Queen* took cover and waited out long minutes, there was nothing to indicate they had been heard.

''They can't be here,'' Kosti said as he crept out of cover at Wilcox's signal.

''Probably haven't been here for some time,'' Rip observed. ''I knew he wasn't a real archaeologist!''

''What about Ali's com?'' cut in Dane. Tang *had* got that faint fix from this general direction—though it was true that the ruins had not been pinpointed as the source of the faint cast-beam.

Wilcox made a long survey of their surroundings. Before them the gap in the ground had been filled in with wreckage until a bridge of uncertain stability faced the crawler. Its ''memory'' had brought them there so it must have crossed here during the trips to carry Rich's supplies. They would have to take the chance and go on if they wanted to know what had become of the archaeologists.

The astrogator started the motor and then clung

with iron fingers as the machine under him bucked and heaved over the loose bridge stuff. Once the treads hit a pocket and the crawler canted to the left. A foot more and it would have spilled its passenger down into the black depths of the gulf.

Kosti went next, both hands on the rope which still tied him to the machine. He took tiny steps in the middle of the bridge, and beneath his helmet drops of sweat washed the fog slick from his cheeks. The others picked their way slowly, testing each step. The fact that they could not see the bottom of the crevice on either side did not make the trip any easier.

Beyond, the crawler picked up speed again and made a quick turn back to its original course. The lifting of the mist was even more apparent—though it did not vanish entirely. But their range of vision, from a foot or two about their persons, had increased to half a block.

"They did have bubble tents," Dane said suddenly. "And regulation camping gear."

"So—where's the camp?" Rip sounded almost peevish. Since he had found the crax cud his buoyant good humor had vanished.

"They wouldn't camp in the city." Dane was convinced of that. There was about these ruins an alien, brooding atmosphere which dragged at one's spirits. He had never regarded himself as a particularly sensitive person, but he felt this strongly. And he believed that the others did also. Little Mura had hardly spoken since they had sighted the ruins, he had dragged back on his guide rope, his eyes darting from one side of the street to the other as if at any

123

moment he expected some formless horror to dash at him out of the murk. Who would dare to set up a tent here, sleep, eat, and carry on the business of daily living fenced in with the age old effluvium which clung to the blasted and broken dwellings—dwellings which perhaps had never harbored human creatures at all?

The crawler drew them on through the maze until the structures which still had a semblance of completeness were behind them once again and only broken walls and shattered mounds of blocks and earth made obstructions around which their machine led them in the pattern it must follow.

It was halfway around one towering mound when Wilcox brought it to a quick stop by smashing his hand down on the control button. That gesture and the frantic haste in which he made it were not lost on the others. They dived into hiding and then began working forward to edge in behind the crawler.

From a cleared space arose—though its lines were still blurred by the fog—a bubble tent, its puffed surface slick with the moisture. They had reached Rich's camp at last.

But Wilcox gave no order to advance. Though they had nothing but suspicion against the archaeologist, the attitude of the astrogator suggested that he was about to reconnoiter a position held by open enemies.

He tightened his helmet strap after adjusting his throat mike. But his orders did not come audibly—instead he gestured them out to encircle the sealed bubble. Dane crept to the right with Rip, automatically keeping cover between them and the tent.

They had gone a quarter of the circle when Rip's hand came down on Dane's arm and the astrogator-apprentice motioned that Thorson was to remain where he was while Rip crawled on to another vantage point in the circle they were drawing about Rich's headquarters.

Dane studied the lay of the ground between his station and the bubble. Here the rubble had been leveled off, packed down, as if the men who camped here needed room to accommodate either crawlers or flitters. But as far as Dane could see, and he was frankly ignorant of the archaeologist's trade, there was no indication of work on uncovering the ruins. Vague memories of items he had seen on news tapes, and Rip's briefings, were his only guides. But surely they should have come across excavations, things waiting for study, maybe even crates ready to pack with transportable finds. But this place had rather the stripped look of a field headquarters for some action team of pioneers or Survey. Could it be left by Survey and not Rich's camp at all?

Then he saw the crawler come into sight, Wilcox on it, his lame leg drawn up so that the fact that he was inactive would not be apparent to anyone watching from the bubble. The crawler crunched on toward the tent without rousing any sign of life within.

But to the astonishment of Dane and the surprise of Wilcox—judging by his expression—the machine did not come to a stop at the level space before the tent. Instead it changed course to evade the bubble and kept steadily on until Wilcox halted it. The astrogator stared at the tent and then his voice whispered in Dane's earphones:

"Come on in—but take it slow!"

They converged on the bubble, slipping from cover and racing across the clearing to new protections. But the tent might be deserted for all the attention their actions aroused. Mura reached the structure first, his sensitive fingers searching for the sealing catch. When the flap peeled down, all of them stared in.

The bubble was only an empty shell. None of its interior partitions had been put into place, even the tilo-floor was missing, so that bare rubble of the field showed. And there was not a box or bag of all the supplies which had been brought from the *Queen* present in that wide space.

"A fake!" Kosti sputtered. "This was set up just to make us think——"

"That they were still here," Wilcox finished for him. "Looks that way, doesn't it?"

"Passing over here in a flitter," Rip murmured, "we'd believe everything was just as it should be. But where *are* they?"

Mura resealed the bubble's flap. "Not here," he announced as if that were a new discovery. "But, Mr. Wilcox, did not the crawler attempt to proceed past this area? Perhaps it knows far more than we have given it credit for——"

Wilcox fingered the throat strap of his helmet. About them the fog was fading—though far more slowly than it had descended. His eyes went from the bubble to the mist beyond. Perhaps if Ali had not been involved he would have ordered a return to the *Queen*. But now, after a pause, he switched on the crawler's motor once more.

The machine circled around the bubble and kept on. There were clumps of vegetation appearing now—the tough grass, the stunted bushes. And knots of rock slanting up signaled their approach to the foothills.

Here the fog which was thinning on the plains curdled again, shutting down until they bunched about the crawler in a tight cluster, each man within arms-distance of his fellows.

That feeling of being spied upon, of being dogged by something they could not see grew strong once more. Under foot the ground became rougher. But Kosti pointed out other tracks, rutted in the soft patches of soil, indications that they were on a road the crawler had used before.

As the mist thickened they strained ears and eyes—but they saw nothing but each other and their machine guide. And what they heard they could not believe.

"Look out!" Rip grabbed at Dane, jerking him back just in time to avoid a painful meeting with a rock wall which loomed out of the fog. From the echo of their boots on the ground they gained the impression that they were entering a narrow defile. Linking hands they spread out—to discover that the four of them marching at arms-length could span the road they now followed.

Once more Wilcox slowed to a halt. He was uneasy. Marching blind this way, they could walk into a trap. On the other hand those they hunted must believe that the crew of the *Queen* would not attempt to travel through the fog. The astrogator had to weigh the possibility of a surprise descent upon the unseen enemy against the chance that he was going into an ambush.

And being imbued with that extra amount of caution which made him an excellent astrogator, Wilcox was not given to snap decisions. Those with him knew that no argument could move him once his mind had been made up. Therefore they sighed with relief when he started the crawler once more.

But the strange solution to their chase came so shortly that it was a shock. For, within feet, they were fronted by towering rock, rock against which the crawler stubbed its flat nose, as its treads continued to bite into the ground as if to force it into the solid, unmoving stone.

10   THE WRECK

"SHE'S TRYING to dig into *that!*" Kosti marveled.

Wilcox snapped out of his surprise and turned off the motor so that the crawler stopped heaving, nuzzling the rock wall through which its "memory" urged it.

"They must have put a false set of co-ordinates on purpose," suggested Rip.

But Dane, remembering that earlier trail which had ended in the same fashion, stepped around Shannon and pressed his palms against the slimy, wet surface of the rock. He was right!

Fainter than it had been in that other valley, the vibration crept up his arms into his body. Not only that, but it was building up, growing in strength even as he stood there. He could feel it now in the ground, striking through the soles of his boots. And the others caught it too.

"What in the—!" exploded Wilcox who hitched forward on the crawler to copy the experiment. "This stuff must be hollow—that installation Tang talked about——"

That was it, of course, the installation which the

com-tech was sure must rival Terra's largest computer, was broadcasting—not only in the sound waves
picked up on the *Queen,* but through the stuff of
Limbo itself! But what was that vast power being
used for and why? And what was the trick which
could send a crawler through solid rock? For Dane
did not agree with Rip that the radar guide had been
tampered with. If that had been done it would have
been more sensible to set it on a point far out in the
barrens, leading any would-be trackers into the
midst of nowhere.

"There's a trick in this—" Wilcox muttered as he
moved his hand with patting motions across the
stone.

But Dane was sure that the astrogator was not
going to spring any hidden latch that way. His own
examination of that other wall in the bright light of
day had taught him the futility of such a hunt.

Kosti leaned against one of the caterpillar treads of
the crawler. "If it went through there once, it isn't
going to do it now. We don't know how to open the
right door. A stick of thorlite might just get us in."

"Now that's a course I *can* compute, man" Rip
hunkered down, running his hands along the ground
line of that exasperating cliff. "How big a stick
would do it, do you think?"

But Wilcox shook his head. "You don't lift a ship
without co-ordinates. Here," he swung to Kosti,
"link com-units with me and let's see if with double
power we can raise the *Queen.*"

The jetman unhooked the energy core of his helmet com and joined it to Wilcox's in an emergency
linkage.

"The installation is picking up voltage," Dane warned, judging by the vibration singing through his finger tips. "Do you think you can break through the interference, sir?"

"That's a thought." Wilcox pulled at his mike. "But they've never been on steady. We can wait for a break in their broadcast."

Rip and Mura came back to the wall. The vibration was a steady beat. Dane walked along to the right. He found a corner where the narrow valley went on—masked by the fog. And he was sure that as he shuffled along, his hand against the stone as a guide, that beat grew stronger. Could one by the sense of touch trace the installation? That was something to think about. What if they unfastened the ropes which had linked them to the crawler and made one long cord of them—an anchorage for a man to explore northeast? He retraced his path and reported to Wilcox, adding his suggestion.

"We'll see what the Captain says," was the astrogator's answer.

The chill which was a part of the fog struck into them now that they were halted. Dane wondered how long Wilcox proposed to linger there. But through their touch on the wall they became aware that the beat of that distant discharge or energy was lessening, that one of the silent intervals was at hand. Wilcox, his fingers on the wall, adjusted the mike with his other hand, determined to make contact the first instant that he could.

And when all but the faintest rumble was gone from the rock, he spoke swiftly in the verbal shorthand of the Traders. Their discoveries among the ruins were reported, as was the present impasse.

There followed an anxious wait. They might be out of range of the *Queen,* even using the stepped-up com. But at last, through the crackle of static, their orders reached them—to make a short exploration along the valley if they wished. But to start back to the ship within the hour.

Wilcox was helped from the crawler before they manhandled the unwieldy vehicle around the re-set its dial for the return journey. Then they tied the ropes into two longer lines for the explorers' use.

Dane did not wait for orders—after all, this was his project. He knotted one of those lines about his middle, leaving his hands free. Just as matter-of-factly Kosti took up the other, almost out of Rip's hands, nor did the jetman pay any attention to Shannon's protests.

"It's starting up again," Mura reported from beside the cliff.

Dane put his left hand on the wall and started off, with Kosti falling into step. They rounded the bend Dane had discovered into the continuation of the valley which was still packed with the cotton wool of the fog.

It was plain that no crawler had ever advanced this far. The narrow way was choked with piles of loose debris over which they helped each other to keep their footing. And the vibration in the wall grew stronger as they went.

Kosti thumped his fist against the stone as they paused for a breather.

"Those drums—they sure keep it up."

132

The distant beat did carry with it some of the roll of a heavy drum.

"Kinda like the Storm Dancers on Gorbe—just a little. And that's devilish stuff, gets into your blood 'til you want to get out and prance along with them. This—well, it's nasty down deep—plain nasty. And you get to believing something's waiting out there—" the jetman's hand indicated the fog, "just waiting to pounce!"

They kept on, climbing now as each ridge of rubble they surmounted was a little higher than the preceding one. They must have been well above the surface of the valley where they had left the crawler when they came upon the strangest find of all.

Dane, clinging to an outcrop in the wall to retain his balance, teetered on the top of a mound. His boot slipped and he tumbled forward before Kosti could snatch him back, rolling down until he brought up with a brusing bump against a dark object. Under his clawing hands he felt, not the rough gravel and earth of the valley, but something else—a smooth sleekness— Had he come upon another ruined building this far from the city?

"Are you hurt?" Kosti called from above. "Look out, I'm coming down."

Dane backed away from his find as Kosti came down feet first in a slide, his boots ringing against that buried thing with the unmistakable clang of metal.

"What the—!" The jetman was on his knees, feeling over that exposed surface. And he was able to identify it. "A ship!"

"What?" Dane crowded in. But now he was able to see the curve of the plates, various other familiar details. They *had* come upon the wreckage of a crash—a bad crash. The ship had jammed its way into the narrow neck of the valley as if it were a cork pounded into a bottle. If they were to go any farther they would have to climb over it. Dane took up his helmet mike and reported the find to the three at the crawler.

"The wreck of that ship you heard coming in?" Wilcox wanted to know. But Dane had seen enough to know that it was not.

"No, sir. This has been here a long time—almost buried and there's rust eaten in. Years since this one lifted, I think——"

"Stay where you are—we're coming up!"

"You can't bring the crawler, sir. Footing is bad."

In the end they did come, supporting Wilcox over the worst bits, keeping contact with the crawler by rope only. In the meantime Kosti prowled around and over the wreck, trying to find a hatch.

"It's a rim prospector of a sort," he reported as soon as Wilcox was settled on a rock to view the find. "But there's something odd about it. I can't name the type. And it's been rooted here a good time. That hatch ought to be about here." He kicked at a pile of loose gravel which banked in one side of the metal hulk. "I think we could dig in."

Rip and Dane returned to the crawler and got the pioneer tools, always kept lashed to the under-carriage of that vehicle. With the shovel and lever they came back to work, taking turns at clearing the debris of years.

"What did I tell you!" Kosti was exultant as a black arc which must mark the top of an open hatch was uncovered.

But it was necessary to shift a lot more of the native soil of Limbo before any one of them could crawl into that hole. Rim prospectors were notoriously sturdy ships, if not swift travelers. They had to be designed to withstand conditions which would shatter liners or disturb even the crack freight- and mail-ships of the Companies.

And the condition of this one proved that its unknown builder had wrought even better than he had hoped. For the smash of its landing had not broken it into bits. Its carcass still hung together, although parts were telescoped.

Kosti leaned on the shovel after he threw out the last scoop of earth. "I can't place it——" He shook his head as if his inability to identify the type of ship worried him.

"How could anyone?" demanded Rip impatiently. "She's nothing but a scrap heap."

"I've seen 'em smashed worse than this." Kosti sounded annoyed. "But the structure—it's wrong——"

Mura smiled. "Rather I would say, Karl, that it is right. I know of no modern ship which could so well survive the landing this one made."

"'No modern ship'?" Wilcox seized upon that. "You have seen one like this before then?"

Mura's smile grew broader. "If I had seen one

such as this plying its trade—then I would be five hundred, perhaps eight hundred years old. This resembles the Class Three, Asteroid Belt ships. There is one, I believe, on display in the Trade Museum at Terraport East. But how it came here—" he shrugged.

Dane's historical cramming had not covered the fine points of ship design, but Kosti and Rip both understood the significance of that, and so did Wilcox.

"But," the astrogator was the first to protest, "they didn't have hyper-drive five hundred years ago. We were still confined to our own solar system——"

"Except for a few crazy experimenters," Mura corrected.

"There are Terran colonies in other systems which are over a thousand years old, you know that. And the details of their flights are sagas in themselves. There were those who went out to cross the gap in frozen sleep, and those who lived for four, six, and eight generations in ships before their far off descendants trod the worlds their ancestors had set course for. And there were earlier variations of the hyper-drive, some of which may have worked, though their inventors never returned to Terra to report success. How an Asteroid prospector came to Limbo I can not tell you. But it has been here a very long time, that I will swear to."

Kosti flashed his torch into the hole they had uncovered. "We can get in—at least for a way——"

Before the smash the prospector had been a small

ship with painfully confined quarters. Compared to her the *Queen* was closer to a liner. And Kosti had to turn back at the inner hatch, unable to squeeze his bulk through the jammed door space. In the end Mura and Dane alone were able to force a path to what had been a combined storage and living quarters.

But under the beam of their torches a fact was immediately clear. A great gap through which soil shifted faced them. This section had been ripped open on the other side, the hole later buried by a slide. But the smash had not done that, the marks of a flamer were plain on the metal. Sometime after its crack-up the prospector had been burnt open, the reason plain. For the portion where they now stood had been stripped—although the traces of cargo containers were on the floor and along the crumpled walls.

"Looted!" Dane exclaimed as the light swept from floor to wall.

To his right was the telescoped section which must have contained the control cabin. There, too, were signs of the flamer but the unknown looters had had little luck beyond. For the holes revealed a mixture of rock and twisted metal which could never be salvaged. Everything forward of the one cargo section they stood in was a total loss.

Mura fingered that slit in the wall. "This was done some time ago—maybe even years. But I think that it was done a long, long time after the ship crashed."

"Why did they want to get in here?"

"Curiosity—a desire to see what she was carrying. A prospector on a long course is apt to make surprising discoveries. And this ship must have had something worth the taking. It was looted. Then, so lightened, the wreckage may have turned over, perhaps earthquakes resettled it and buried it more completely. But it was looted——''

''You don't think that the survivors of its crew may have returned? They could have taken off in an escape flitter before the crash——''

''No, there was too long a time between the crash and the looting. This ship was discovered by some-one else and stripped. I do not think that they—'' Mura pointed to the fore-compartment, ''escaped.''

Did Limbo have intelligent inhabitants, natives who could use a flamer to cut through ship alloy? But the globe things—Dane refused to believe that those queer creatures had looted the prospector.

Before they climbed out of the ship Mura pushed as far as he could into the fore-section. And when he inched out again he was repeating a number.

''Xc—4 over 9532600,'' he said. ''Her registry, by some chance it is still visible. Remember that: Xc—4 over 9532600.''

But Dane was interested in another point. ''That's Terran registry!''

''I suspected that it would be. She is Asteroid class—perhaps an experimental ship with one of the very early hyper-drives. She might have been a pri-vate ship, the work of one or two men, an attempt to pioneer in a new direction. Could that tangle ever be uncoiled our engineers ought to discover some in-teresting alternate of the usual engine. It could be worth the effort to break through just for that——''

"Ahoy!" the voice from the outer air summoned. "What are you doing in there?"

Dane spoke into his mike, outlining what they had found. Then they squeezed out through the hatch.

"Stripped bare!" Kosti was openly disappointed. "Opened up and stripped bare. She must have been carrying something really worthwhile for all the trouble they took to do it."

"I'd rather know who stripped her. Even if it was done years ago," was Rip's comment and it was evident that Wilcox agreed with him.

The astrogator pulled himself to his feet, leaning against a rock. "We'd better get back to the *Queen*."

Dane glanced around. He was sure that the fog was thinning here as it had back around the ruins. If it would just clear—then they could take up a flitter and really comb this district! They had discovered no trace of Ali anywhere, and each step they took seemed to plunge them only deeper into mystery.

Rich and his party had vanished—into a stone wall if the crawler was to be relied upon. Now here was a ship which had been looted long after it had crashed. And somewhere deep in the heart of Limbo beat an unknown installation which might offer the worst threat of all!

They went back to the crawler and by the time Wilcox was once more established on it, the fog was retreating, more swiftly now. As it lifted they read on the scraped walls, in the rutted soil that this was or had been a thoroughfare in good use. Those who had come and gone this path had made it a lane of travel before and arrival of the *Queen*, some of those marks were far more than a few days old.

Survey's tapes had said nothing of all this—the ruins, the installation, the wrecked ships. Why not? Had Survey's report been edited? But Limbo had been put up to legal auction just as usual. Did it mean that Survey's scout teams had not explored this continent to any extent—that seeing the evidences of a burn-off their investigation had been only superficial?

It was raining now, a drizzle which worked into the high collars of their tunics and soaked the upper linings of their boots. Unconsciously their pace quickened as the crawler took the homeward trundle. Dane wished that there was some way they could cut cross country and shorten the march which lay between them and the *Queen*. But at least they no longer had to rope themselves to the carrier.

They came into the ruins again, maintaining a careful watch for any signs of life there. The brilliant hues of the buildings were subdued by the lack of sunlight, but they still warred with one another and jolted Terran senses in a subtle fashion. Either the people who had built this city had a different type of vision, or a chemical reaction from the burn-off had altered the color schemes for the worse. As it was, none of the Traders felt exactly comfortable if they looked too long at those walls.

"It isn't altogether the color—" Rip spoke aloud. "It's their shape, too. Those angles are wrong—just enough wrong to be disturbing——"

"The burn-off blast may have shaken them up," offered Dane. But Mura was not ready to accept that.

"No, Rip has it right. The colors, they are wrong for us, also the shapes. See that tower—over there? Only three floors remain, but once it was taller. Let your eyes rise along the lines of those floors into space—where once must have been other walls. It is all wrong—those lines——"

Dane saw what he meant. With imagination one could add more floors to the tower—but when one did! For a moment he was dizzy as he tried that feat. It was very easy, after studying all this, to believe that the Forerunners had been alien, alien beyond any race that the Terrans, new come to the Galactic lanes, had encountered.

He hurriedly averted his eyes from that tower, winced as his gaze swept across an impossibly scarlet foundation and fastened with relief on the comfortable monotone of the crawler and Wilcox's square back in the drab brown Service tunic.

But the astrogator had not joined his companions in their speculations concerning their surroundings. He was hunched over, both hands clutching the mike of the stepped-up com Kosti had not yet altered. And there was something in his posture which altered the others as they watched him.

11 SARGASSO WORLD

DANE STRAINED to hear a hint of sound in his helmet phones. There was a far off click which faded quickly. But it was evident that Wilcox with his double powered com received more than that.

The astrogator took one hand from the mike and gestured the others to come to the stalled crawler. Luckily no drone from the interference blanketed the air waves. And by some freak the word "stay" boomed suddenly in Dane's ears.

Wilcox looked up at them. "We're not to go back now——"

"What's wrong?" Mura's voice lost none of its mild tone.

"The *Queen*'s surrounded——"

"Surrounded!" "By whom?" "What happened?" the questions came together in a confused gabble.

"They were fired upon when they tried to leave the ship. And there's some reason why they can't lift. We're to keep clear until they can find out what's behind it all——"

Mura glanced over his shoulder at the valleys now

unveiled as the mist drifted away in tattered streamers.

"If we cut across the open," he said slowly, "we can be seen with ease now that the fog is gone. But suppose we go back—along the valley mouths, paralleling the burnt-off country. We should reach a point opposite the *Queen,* and then we can climb the heights until we are able to see what is going on about her——"

Wilcox nodded. "We're not to try contact by com. They're afraid we might be picked up."

Though the fog had lifted visibility was not good. It must be well into evening and the astrogator surveyed their present surroundings with disfavor. It was plain that they could not move through the rough foothill country in the dark. Their travels must wait until morning. But he did not order them to find shelter in the city buildings. Mura broke the short silence first.

"There is the bubble—we could camp there for the night. I do not think it has been used since it was erected as a blind."

They seized upon that thankfully and the crawler made the return trip to the abandoned camp of the archaeologists. They unsealed the full door flap, allowing their carrier space to enter. And when the portal was closed again Dane had a feeling of relief. The walls enclosing them were Terran made, he had slept in such shelters before. And that familiarity was in a measure security against the alien quality of the city without.

The bubble cut off the night winds and they were not too uncomfortable in spite of the lack of heat.

Kosti who had been wandering about the hollow shell kicked at an inoffensive bit of rock.

"They could have left the heating unit. That's supposed to be part of one of these———"

Rip laughed. "But they didn't know we were coming."

Kosti stared at him, inclined to be affronted, and then he chuckled.

"No, they did not know. We can't complain—" his deep roar of laughter was directed at himself.

Mura busied himself with duties which were part of his usual job, collecting their emergency rations and parceling out to each one of the tasteless cubes and so many sips from their canteens. Dane wondered at the steward's careful measurements. It was as if Mura did not believe they were going to return to the *Queen* in the near future and thought that these limited supplies might have to last for a long time.

Once they had eaten, they drew together for warmth, stretching out on the bare floor. Outside the bubble they could hear the moan of the night winds, rising to a crescendo of weird cries as it wailed through fissures of the ruins.

Dane's thoughts were restless. What was wrong with the *Queen?* If the ship was besieged why hadn't she simply lifted from the landing and set down elsewhere, giving them directions where to join her, or sending out the flitter to pick them up? What kept the freighter planet bound?

Perhaps the others shared his worries, but there were no speculations voiced in the dark, no questions asked. Having their orders they had determined upon a course of action for themselves and now they were getting what rest they could.

Shortly after dawn the haggard Wilcox sat up and then limped to the crawler. In the pinched gray light he looked years older and there was a tight set to his lips as he bent over the machine, making the adjustments which would leave it on manual control during the hours to come.

None of them could have been asleep for Wilcox's action acted as a signal and they were all on their feet, stretching the cramp out of arms and legs. Greetings were grunts as they ate what Mura allowed them. Then they were out in the crispness of the morning. Streaks of color heralded the sun they had not seen for so long and the last of the fog was gone. In the north the mountains were stark and bare against the sky.

Wilcox pointed the crawler north where the foothill valleys pushed out in a ragged fringe. There was plenty of cover there and they could slip east undetected. Of them all the astrogator had the most difficult job. Here was no smooth path for the crawler. And within a half mile he had to throttle down to a slow walking pace or be bounced from his seat.

In the end they separated into two parties. Two of them at a time scouted ahead, while the two remaining stayed with Wilcox and the crawler at the slower pace. From all signs they might have been alone in a dead world. No tracks broke the soil, there were no sounds, and they did not even sight one of the rare insects which must keep to the more hospitable inner portions of the valleys.

Dane was on advance patrol with Mura when the steward gave a grunt and raised his hands as if to shade his eyes. Above them the sun had struck fire from some gleaming surface, struck it strong enough to flash a burning beam down at the Terrans.

"Metal!" Dane cried. Could this be another clue to the installation?

He started toward that spot, first clambering with difficulty over the debris left by a recent slide of small rocks. Then he pulled himself up on a ledge the slide had uncovered and made his way to the source of that flash. What he expected he did not really know. But what he found was wreckage—wreckage of another space ship—although the outlines were strange, even allowing for alterations made by the force of its landing. It was smaller than the prospector they had discovered the day before, and in a greater state of disintegration, the parts which had been exposed before the slide brought it all to the surface were only rust-eaten scraps.

Mura joined him and looked down at the crumpled thing which had once navigated space.

"This is old—very, very old." He tried to pick up a rod shaped bit. Between his fingers it became red dust. "Old—I do not think a Terran ever flew this one."

"A Forerunner ship?" Dane was startled. If that were true—this *was* a find—a find which might bring Survey and its kindred services back to Limbo with all jets blazing.

"Not that old—or it would not exist. But the Rigellians and that vanished race of Angol Two were in Galactic space before we were. This may be an

146

ancient vessel of their building. It is so very old——"

"What brought it here?" Dane wondered. "That was a smash landing, and the prospector ended the same way. Then there was that ship we heard come in before the fog closed down. Yet the *Queen* didn't have any trouble making a good landing. I don't get it. One crack up—but three——?"

"It makes one think," Mura agreed. "Perhaps we should look about a bit more. The solution to this puzzle may lie within sight and sound and yet we are not clever enough to learn it."

They waited on the ledge until they could signal to the slowly advancing party with the crawler. The astrogator took careful bearings on the site. If and when they had time, they might later send a party to explore this discovery—since its age and alien origin might make it of value.

"This reminds me somehow," Kosti said, "of how those Sissiti catch the purple lizards they make boots of. They set up a thing that waggles back and forth—just a thin wire attached to a motor. But the lizard sees it and—pow—he's sunk. Sits there watching that stupid thing wiggle-waggle until a Sissit comes along and pops him into a bag. Maybe someone's set up a wiggle-waggle here to draw in ships—that would be something!"

Wilcox stared at him. "Could be you have something at that," he replied, as he fingered his mike. It was apparent he longed to report this second find to the *Queen*. And he had a suggestion for the scouting parties. "Take a look up these valleys if you can without wasting too much time. I'd like to know if

147

there are any more wrecks strewn about in this general area.''

So from then on, though they continued to work their way east to flank the *Queen*, they also made side trips into the valleys for short distances. And it was Kosti and Rip who found the third ship.

Where the two other shattered discoveries had been of an earlier day, this was not only of their own time but a type of craft they were able to recognize at once. Through some freak its disastrous ending had not been as bad as those which had telescoped the prospector and smashed the alien. While the new find lay on its side showing buckled and broken plates, it was not crushed.

''Survey.'' Rip yelled almost before they were within hearing distance.

There was no reason to mistake the insignia on the battered nose—the crossed, tailed comets were as well known along the star trails as the jagged lightning swords of the Patrol.

Wilcox limped forward with the rest as they trailed along its length.

''The hatch is open—'' Rip called down from the pinnacle he had climbed for a better look.

It was what dangled from that open hatch which centered their attention. A rope hanging like that could mean only one thing—that there had been survivors! Was this the explanation for all the puzzling happenings on Limbo? Dane tried to remember how many men comprised the crew of a Survey ship—they usually had a group of specialists— perhaps as many as rode in the *Queen*—perhaps more——

Though there was no reason why anyone would have remained in the wrecked ship, the men from the *Queen* prepared to explore. Rip dropped from the pinnacle and balanced across to that hatch. Only Wilcox had to remain where he was as the others climbed the rope.

It was a strange experience to lower oneself down a well which was once a corridor, Dane found. Ahead, torches picked out fugitive gleams from smooth surfaces as the explorers poked into the cabins.

"She's been stripped!" Rip's words rang in the helmet coms back along the line. "I'm for control——"

Dane knew very little of the geography of a Survey ship. He could only follow the others, halting at the first open panel to peer inside with the aid of his own torch. This must have been the storage for space suits and exploring gear as it was on the *Queen*. But it was empty now—cupboards gaping as if their contents had been hurriedly ripped loose. Had the crew left the boat in space before the crash? No, that did not explain the rope.

"Lord above us!" The shock in that cry stopped Dane where he was. Rip's voice in the com was so strained, horrified— What *had* the other discovered in the control section?

"What's the matter?" that was Wilcox, impatient at being left out.

"Coming——" Kosti's growl came next.

And a few moments later the jetman's voice was loud with a crackle of expletives as shocked as Rip's exclamation had been.

"What *is* it?" fumed Wilcox.

Dane left the storage space and made his way quickly to the passageway tying together all sections of the ship, which should lead him directly to what the others had found. Mura was ahead of him there and he soon caught up with the steward.

"We've found them," Rip's voice was bleak and old as he answered the astrogator.

"Found who?" Wilcox wanted to know.

"The crew!"

The passage ahead of Dane was blocked. He could see past Mura, but Kosti's bulk and Rip's shut out what lay beyond. Then Rip spoke again and Dane hardly knew it for his voice.

"Got—to—get—out—of—here——"

"Yes!" that was Kosti.

Both of them turned and Mura and Dane had to retrace their way to the hatch, hurried on by the impatience of the two behind them. They climbed out on the curving side of the ship, giving way to the others. Rip crawled down toward the fins. He held fast to the braces of one and proceeded to be thoroughly sick.

Kosti's face was greenish, but he maintained control with a visible effort. None of the other three quite dared at that moment to ask what either man had seen. It wasn't until Rip, shivering, crept back and slid down the rope to the ground that Wilcox lost patience.

"Well, what happened to them?"

"Murder!" Rip's voice rang too loudly, echoed by some freak of the stone abutments about them until "Murrrderrr" was shouted in their ears.

Dane glanced around in time to see Mura descend again into the ship. In the shadow of his helmet the small man's face was composed and he gave no reason for his return.

Nor did Wilcox ask any more questions. After a minute or two Mura's voice sounded in their coms.

"This ship has also been stripped by loot-ers——"

First the prospector hulk and then this—which must have been far more rewarding. Survivors of earlier crashes could have been searching for supplies, for material to make life more endurable but—Rip had an answer to that line of thought and he gave it in a single outburst:

"The Survey men were blaster burned!"

Blaster burned! Just as the globe things had been killed in that valley. Ruthless cruelty of a sort un-known to the civilized space lanes was in power on Limbo. Then another announcement from Mura electrified them all.

"This, I believe, is the missing *Rimbold!*"

The Survey ship whose disappearance had indi-rectly led to the auction on Naxos, and so their own arrival on Limbo! But how had it reached here and what had brought it crashing down on this world? Survey ships, because of the nature of their duty, were as nearly foolproof as any ships could be. In a hundred years perhaps two had been lost. Yet the *Rimbold*, for all of its safety devices and the drilled know-how of its experienced crew, had been as luckless as the earlier ships they had discovered.

Dane slid down on the rope, Kosti following him. The sun had gone under a cloud and there was a spatter of rain on the rocks about. It was thickening into a drizzle as the steward joined them. Whatever he had seen within the *Rimbold,* it had not upset him as completely as it had Rip and Kosti. Instead he had a thoughtful, almost puzzled look.

"Does not Van tell a story like this?" he asked suddenly. "It is one from the old days when ships rode the sea waves, not the star lanes. Then there was said to be a place in a western ocean of our own earth where no winds blew and a weed grew thick, trapping within it the ships of those days so that they were matted together into a kind of floating land of decay and death——"

Rip's attention was caught, Dane saw him nod. "The Sago—no—the Sargasso Sea!"

"That is so. Here, too, we have something like—a Sargasso of space which in some way traps ships, bringing them in to smash against its rocks and be held forever captive. And whatever it is must have great power. This Survey ship is no experimental prospector of the early days when calculations were faulty and engines could easily fail."

"But," Wilcox protested, "the *Queen* made a routine landing without any trouble at all!"

"Did it occur to you," Mura said, "that she might have been permitted to make such a landing—for a reason——"

That would explain a great many things, but the idea was chilling. It suggested that the *Solar Queen* was a pawn in someone's game—Rich's? And that she no longer had any control over her destiny.

"Let's get along!" Wilcox shifted his weight and

started limping back to where they had left the crawler.

And from then on they made no more side expeditions hunting wrecks. There were probably more of them to be found, Dane suspected. Mura's idea had taken hold of his imagination—a Sargasso of space, drawing into its clutch wanderers of the lanes which came into the area of its baleful influence—whatever that influence could be. Why had the *Queen* been able to make a normal landing on a world where other ships crashed? Was it because they had had Rich and his men on board? Who and what was Rich?

They splashed through a stream which had been fed by the rain. It was there that Wilcox pulled up the crawler and spoke: "We must be getting close to a point opposite the *Queen*. If we don't want to miss her we should get aloft—" He pointed to the cliff.

In the end it was decided to make temporary camp with the crawler for their base, leaving Wilcox and two others there, while two more in turn climbed the heights and scouted ahead. It was now past noon and with the coming of night they would be able to move freely. So they must discover their vantage point before dark.

Rip and Mura made the first scout, but when Shannon came back to report—since they dared no longer trust to the com-calls which others might catch—it was to say that the *Queen* was in sight but farther ahead.

With caution Wilcox started up the crawler, taking it out of the valley they had just selected, through the rough edge of the plains, until he had gained a mile beyond their first proposed base. Concealed there behind a tall outcrop, he waited for a second report—and this time Mura made it.

"From there," he indicated a pinnacle of rock, "one can see well. The *Queen* is sealed—and there are others around her. As yet we have not had a chance to count them or see their arms——"

Kosti, his fear of the heights still operating to keep him from climbing, had prowled along on the plain. Now he returned with news as much to the point as Mura's.

"There is a place, right up there behind the look-out, where you can park the crawler and it can't be seen from any angle——"

Wilcox headed the machine for that point and the jetman took the astrogator's place to maneuver the crawler into the confined quarters. While Kosti and Wilcox stayed there, Dane climbed with Mura up to the spy post where Rip was already stationed, his back supported by a rock, far-distance glasses to eyes as he faced south, looking out over the burnt-off land.

There was the sky pointing needle of the *Queen*. It was true she was sealed, the ramp was in, the hatch closed, she might have made ready for a blast-off. Dane unhooked his own glasses and adjusted the range until the rocky terrain about the ship's fins leaped up at him.

12 SHIP BESIEGED

EVEN AFTER he had the glasses focused he could not be sure that he saw more than just one strangely shaped vehicle and the two men by it. To Dane's angle of sight the party appeared to be fully exposed to those in the *Queen*. And he wondered why the Traders had not attacked—if this was the enemy.

"Right out in the open—" he said aloud. But Rip was not so sure.

"I don't think so. There's a ridge there. Visibility's poor now, but it would show in sunlight. With a stun rifle——"

Yes, with a stun rifle, and this elevation to aid him, a man might pick off those foreshortened figures—even with the range as great as it was. Unfortunately their full armament now consisted of only shot range weapons—the close-to-innocuous sleep ray rods, and the blasters—potent enough, but only for in-fighting.

"Might as well wish for a bopper while you're about it," Dane commented.

Both flitters had disappeared from the landing place near the ship. He supposed they had been warped in for safety. Now he swept the ground slowly, trying to pick out any shapes which did not seem natural. And within five minutes he was sure he had pinpointed at least as many posts of two or three watchers staked out in an irregular circle about the ship. Four of the groups had transportation—machines which resembled their own crawlers to some degree but were narrower and longer, as if they had been designed to negotiate the valleys of this planet.

"Speaking of boppers," Rip's voice startled Dane because of its tenseness, "what's that? Over there——"

Dane's glasses obediently turned west. "Where?"

"See that rock that looks a little like a hoobat's head—to the left of that."

Dane searched for a rock suggesting Captain Jellico's pet monstrosity. He finally found it. To the left—now. Yes! A straight barrel. Was that—could that be the barrel of a portable bopper, wheeled into a position which commanded the ship, from which it could drop its deadly little eggs right under her fins?

A bopper couldn't begin to make any impression on a sealed ship, that was true. But it could and would bring sudden death to those venturing out into the gas which burst from its easily shattered ammunition. One had to take a bopper seriously.

"Space!" he spit out. "We must have strayed into a darcon's nest——"

"With the clawed one breathing down our necks into the bargain," agreed Rip. "Why doesn't the

156

Queen lift? They could set down anywhere and pick us up later. Why stay boxed in here?''

"Do you not think," asked Mura, "that perhaps the odd behavior of our ship may have something to do with the wrecks? That maybe if the *Queen* takes to the air she might become as they are?"

"I'm no engineer," Dane said, "but I don't see how they could bring her down. They haven't any big stuff lined up out there. It'd take a maul to push her off course———"

"Did you see any signs of an attack by a maul on the *Rimbold?* There were none. She crashed as if she were drawn to this planet by some force she could not resist. Those who wait down there may have the secret of such a force. It could be that they rule not only the surface of Limbo, but some portion of the heavens above———"

"You think that the installation is a part of it?" Rip inquired.

"Who knows?" the steward's quiet voice continued. "It might well be." He was watching the plain through his own glasses. "I would like to slip down there after nightfall and prowl about. If we could have a quiet and informative talk with one of those sentries———"

Mura's tone did not change, he was his usual placid, unexcited self. But Dane knew that the last person he would care to change places with at that particular moment was one of the sentries Mura wished to "talk."

"Hmmm——" Rip was studying the terrain. "It might be done at that. Or a man could get to the *Queen* and find out what this was all about———"

"You don't think we could reach them by com?" suggested Dane. "We're close enough for a clear reception."

"Notice those helmets on the sentries' heads?" Rip pointed out. "I'll bet you earth-side pay that they're linked up on our frequency now. If we talk they'll listen—not only listen but get a fix on us. And they know this ground better than we do. Would you like to play hide and seek across this country in the dark?"

Dane decidedly would not. But it was difficult to relinquish using the coms. So easy to just call and find out what might take hours and hours of spying and risk to discover by themselves. Only, as the Masters had dinned into them for years back in the Pool, there were few easy short cuts in Trade. It was a matter of using your wits from first to last, of being able to improvise on the spur of the moment such dodges as would save your profit, your ship or your skin. And the last two precious articles appeared to be at stake on this occasion.

"At least," Rip was continuing, "we are sure now that more than Rich and his hand-picked boys are involved."

"Yes," Mura nodded, "it would seem that the forces ranged against us are numerically stronger." His glasses coursed from one group of hidden men to the next, until he had made the complete circle concealed from those aboard the *Queen*. "There are perhaps fifteen out there."

"To say nothing of reinforcements they may have back in the mountains. But who in the Black Reaches

158

of Outer Space are they?'' Rip asked of the air about them.

"Something is about to happen.'' Mura stiffened, his attention settling on one spot.

Dane followed the steward's lead. The other was right. One of the besiegers had walked boldly out of cover and now approached the ship, waving vigorously over his head the age-old sign for parley—a strip of white cloth.

For a moment or two it appeared as if the *Queen* was not going to answer that. And then the hatch opened far above the surface of the ground. No ramp was lowered. Instead a figure paused in the opening and Dane recognized Captain Jellico.

The bearer of the white flag hesitated some distance away. Though the watchers could not see too clearly in the growing dusk, they could hear, for a voice crackled in their helmet phones, thus proving Rip right—the coms of the raiders were on the same band as their own.

"Thought it over, Captain? Ready to be sensible?''

"Is that all you want to know?'' Jellico's rasp could not be mistaken. "I gave you my decision last night."

"You can sit here until you starve, Captain. Just try to get off-world——''

"If we can't get off—neither can you get in!''

"And there he speaks the truth,'' Mura observed. "Nothing they have down there is capable of forcing an entrance to the *Queen*. And if they are able to smash her—she will be of no use to them.''

"You think that that is what they are after—the *Queen?*" hazarded Dane.

Rip snorted. "That's obvious. They don't want her to lift—they have a use for her. I'll bet that Rich brought us here just to get the *Queen.*"

"There is the matter of supplies, Captain," the besieger's voice purred in their earphones. "We can afford to sit here half a year if it is necessary—you can not! Come, do not be so childish. We have offered you a fair deal all around. And you have been caught in a pinch, have you not? Your ready funds went at the auction when you bought trading rights here. Well, we are offering you better than trading rights. And we have the patience to sit it out."

But, if the speaker had the patience he vaunted, one of his fellows did not. Through the air came the crack of a stun rifle. Jellico either ducked or fell back into the ship and the hatch was clapped to. The three Traders on the cliff sat very still. It appeared that the man with the flag had not expected that move on the part of his own side. He stayed where he was for a moment before he dropped the treacherous strip of white and dived for the cover of an outcrop, from which point he squirmed back to his original post.

"That was not planned," remarked Mura. "Someone was a fraction impatient. He will suffer for his zeal—since he has just put an end to the chance of future negotiation."

"Do you think the captain was hurt?" Dane asked.

"The old man knows all the tricks." Rip did not seem worried. "I'd say he got out in a hurry. But now they'll have to starve him into surrender. That shot is not going to get our men to come out with their hands up——''

"Meanwhile," Mura dropped his glasses to his knee, "there is the little matter of our own action. We might be able to slip through those lines in the dark, but with the ship sealed, how can we get in? They are not going to lower a line at the first hail out of the night. Not now."

Dane gazed across the rough ground which lay between the heights on which he perched and the distant ship. Yes, it might be simple to avoid the sentry post of the besiegers, they would be more intent on the ship than on the territory behind their own lines. Maybe they did not even know that some of the *Queen*'s crew had escaped their trap. But, having reached the ship, how could one get on board?

"A problem, a problem," Mura murmured.

"Aren't we on a level with the control section here?" Rip asked suddenly. "Maybe we could rig up some kind of a signal to let them know we were sending someone in——"

Dane was willing to try. He squinted along the line from where he sat to the nose of the ship.

"It will have to be done very soon," Mura warned. "Night is coming fast."

Rip looked up at the sky. The sun of the morning had long since vanished. Leaden clouds hung over them. And it was clearly twilight.

"Suppose we make a shelter—maybe out of our tunics—and light a torch in it. The range of the light would be limited at the sides—it could not be seen from below. But those on the *Queen* might catch it——''

The steward's answer was to unbuckle his equipment belt and pull at the seal latch of his tunic. Dane hurriedly followed his example. Then they crouched shivering in the cold, holding their tunics as side screens, while Rip squatted between, flashing his torch on and off in the distress signal of the Trading code. It was such a slim chance, someone would have to be in the control cabin watching at just the right angle to catch that click, click of light—a mere pinprick of radiance.

Then the night beacon of the *Queen* flashed on, striking up into the gray sky as it had fought the fog a day earlier. Only now it lit the surrounding clouds. And as the three on the cliff watched, hoping to read in this some reply to their improvised com, the yellowish beam took on a ruddier tinge.

Mura sighed with relief. "They have read us——''

"How do you know?" Dane could see nothing to lead the steward to believe that.

"They had switched on the storm ray. See, now it fades once more. But they read us!" He was smiling as he donned his tunic. "I would suggest that we compose a proper message among us and also inform Wilcox of this development. If we can communicate with the *Queen,* even if she can not with us, something may be done to our advantage after all."

So they went down to the crawler. It did not take long to relay the news.

"But they can not answer us." Wilcox put his finger on the weakness of the whole set up. "They wouldn't have used the storm ray if they had had any other means of letting us know they read you——"

"We'll have to send someone in. Now we can signal that he is coming and they will be waiting to take him aboard," Rip said eagerly.

Wilcox's manner suggested that he did not wholly agree with that plan. But, though they discussed it point by point, there did not seem to be any other solution.

Mura got to his feet. "The dark is coming fast. We must decide upon a plan at once, for the climb to our signal post is not one to be taken when it can not be seen. Who is to go and when? That much we can send in code——"

"Shannon," Wilcox singled out the astrogator-apprentice, "this is the time those cat's eyes of yours will come in handy. You can see as much in the dark as Sinbad—or you seemed to that time on Baldur. Want to try to make it at, say" he consulted his watch, "twenty-one hours? That will give our play-mates on the sentry posts time to settle down."

Rip's beaming face was answer enough. And he was humming as the three once more ascended the rock and took over the task of beaming the message.

"You will add," Mura remarked, "that your safe arrival is to be signaled back to us with the storm ray. We would like to rejoice in your success."

"Sure, man. But I'm not worrying." Rip's natural buoyance was returning for the first time since he had made that horrible discovery in the wrecked *Rimbold*. "This is a stroll compared to that job we had on Baldur."

Mura looked grave. "Never underestimate what may stand against you. You are experienced enough in Trade to remember that, Rip. This is no time to take unnecessary chances——"

"Not me, man! I'll be as silent and slippery as a snake out there. They will never know I passed by."

Once again the steward and Dane shed their tunics and shivered in the damp cold as Rip flashed the news of his mission across to the silent, sealed ship. There was no answer but they were certain that after their first assay at communication there had been a watcher stationed to wait for a second message.

It was arranged that Mura and Dane were to bed down on the heights while Rip went back to the crawler and waited to set out from there. When the astrogator-apprentice disappeared below, Dane moved rocks to provide them with a windbreak.

They had no source of warmth but their nearness to each other, so they crouched together in the pocket Dane had devised, with nothing to do but wait out the hours until the signal came that Rip had reached his goal.

"Lighting up," Mura murmured.

The beam from the *Queen* still beaconed in the night. But what Mura referred to were the sparks of fire which marked the fixed posts of the unknown sentries.

"Make it easier for Rip—he'll be able to avoid them," ventured Dane but his companion disagreed.

"They will be alert for trouble. Probably they

have beats linking each of those with the rest and are doing sentry-go along them.''

''You mean—they guess that we are here—that they are only waiting for Rip to come along——''

''That may or may not be true. But they are, of course, alert for a move from the men in the *Queen*. Tell me, Thorson, are you not now aware of something more? Can you not feel it through this rock?''

Of course he could. That beat of the installation, less heavy than it had been near the ruins, but faithful in its pattern. And now there was no fluctuation in its power as the long minutes dragged wearily by. It was running steadily at full strength.

''That,'' Mura continued, ''is what ties the *Queen* to this earth——''

The jig-saw bits of what they had learned during the past two days were beginning to fit into a picture. Suppose these strangers who had enmeshed the *Queen* for some purpose of their own, did control a means of crashing her if she tried to lift from Limbo? It would be necessary to keep that installation, energy broadcaster, beam, or whatever it was, working all the time or the ship would make a sneak escape. Those in her must be fitting the pieces together, too—even if they did not yet know the Sargasso properties of Limbo.

''Then the only way to get out of here,'' said Dane slowly, ''is to find the source of power and——''

''Smash it? Yes. If Rip makes contact—then we must move to that end.''

''You say 'if Rip makes contact.' Don't you think he's going to?''

''You are very young in the Service, Thorson.

After some voyages a man becomes very humble. He begins to realize that the quality we name on Terra 'luck' has much to do with success or failure. We can never honestly say that this or that plan of action will come to fruition in the manner we hope, there are too many governing factors over which we have no control. We do not count on any fact until it is an established reality. Shannon has many of the odds on his side. He has unusually keen night sight, a fact we discovered on a similar situation not long ago, he is used to field work, he is not easily confused. And from here he has had a chance to study the territory and the positions of the enemy. The odds are perhaps eighty percent in his favor. But there remains that twenty percent. He must be ready and we must be ready to prepare for other moves—until we see the beacon signal that he has made it.''

Mura's emotionless voice unsettled Dane. It had the old illusion-pricking touch of Kamil, refined, made even more pointed and cutting. Kamil! Where was Ali? Being held by some of those now ranged about the *Queen?* Or had he been taken on to the mysterious source of power?

''What do you suppose they did with Kamil?'' Dane asked aloud.

''He represents to them a source of information about us and our concerns. As such they would see that he reaches the guiding brain behind all this. And he will be safe—just as long as they have a use for him——''

But there was something vaguely sinister in that answer—a hint twisting Dane's memory to a scene he did not like to recall.

166

"Those men on the *Rimbold*— Was Rip right? Had they been blasted?"

"He was right." The three words were unaccented by any emotion, and the very gentleness of the reply made it the more forceful.

They talked very little after that, and only moved about when the warning stiffness of arm or leg made it necessary. On the plain the beacon continued to point starward from ship without change.

In spite of the cold and the cramp, the beat of the vibration was lulling. Dane had to fight to keep awake, using an old trick of recalling in detail one tape after another in the "Rules of Stores" he had made his study during the voyage out. If he were only back in Van Rycke's cubby now, safely engrossed in his studies, with nothing more exciting than a sharp piece of bargaining to look forward to in the morning!

A whistle, low, yet penetrating, reached their ears from the depths. That was Rip, about to set out on his risky venture. Dane held his glasses to his eyes, though he knew very well that he could not follow the other's progress through the dark.

The rest of the hours seemed days long. Dane watched the beacon with a single-minded intensity which made his eyes ache. But there was no change. He felt Mura shift beside him, fumbling in the dark and a faint glow told him that beneath the shelter of tunic hem the other was consulting his watch.

"How long?"

"He has been out four hours——"

Four hours! It wouldn't take a man four hours to reach the *Queen* from here. Even if he had to detour and hide out at intervals to escape the sentries. It looked very much as if that twenty percent which Mura had mentioned as standing against the success of Rip's mission was indeed the part to be dealt with now.

13 ATTACK AND STALEMATE

Dawn was hinted at with a light in the east, and still the *Queen*'s beacon had not changed its hue. The watchers did not expect it to now. Something had gone wrong—Rip had never reached the ship.

Unable to stand inaction longer, Dane crept from the improvised shelter and started along the cliff on which they had set up their lookout. It formed a wall between the entrances to two of the tongue-shaped valleys—the one in which Wilcox and Kosti were encamped, the other unknown territory.

Dane sighted a trickle of stream in the second. The presence of water heralded, or had heralded, other life in his experience of Limbo. And here and now that pattern held. For he counted ten of the small checkerboard spice fields.

But this time the fields were not deserted. Two of the globe creatures worked among the plants. They stirred the ground about the roots of the spice ferns with their thread-like tentacles, their round backs bobbing up and down as they moved.

Then both of them stood upright. Since they lacked any discernible heads or features, it was difficult for Dane to guess what they were doing. But their general attitude suggested that they were either listening or watching.

Three more of the globes came noiselessly into sight. Between two of them swung a pole on which was tied the limp body of an animal about the size of a cat. No audible greeting passed between the hunters and the farmers. But they gathered in a group, dropping the pole. Through the glasses Dane saw that their finger tentacles interlocked from globe to globe until they formed a circle.

"Sooo—" The word hissed out of the early morning murk and Dane, who had been absorbed in the scene below, gave a start, as Mura's hand closed on his shoulder.

"There is a crawler coming this way—" the steward whispered.

Once more the group of globes had an aura of expectancy. They scattered, moving with a speed which surprised the Terrans. In seconds they had taken cover, leaving the fields, the stream bank deserted.

The crunch of treads on loose stone and gravel was clear to hear as a vehicle crept into the vision range of the two on the cliff. Just as Kamil had been the first to discover, the crawler was not the usual type favored by Federation men. It was longer, more narrow, and had a curious flexibility when it moved, as if its body was jointed.

One man sat behind its controls. An explorer's helmet shielded his face, but he wore the same mixture of outer garments as Rich and his men had affected.

Mura's hand on Dane's shoulder applied pressure. But Dane, too, was aware of the trap about to be sprung. Masked by a line of brush, there was stealthy movement. A globe thing came into the Traders' sight, clasping close to its upper ball body a large stone. One of its fellows joined it, similarly armed.

"—trouble." Mura's voice was a thin whisper.

The crawler advanced at a steady pace, crunching over the ground, splashing through the edge of the water. It had reached the first field now, and the driver made no effort to avoid the enclosure. Instead he drove on, the wide treads rolling flat, first the low wall, and then the carefully tended plants that it guarded.

The globe things, hidden from their enemy, scuttling on a course which paralleled that of the vehicle. Their stones were still tightly grasped and they moved with a lightning speed. By all the signs the man on the crawler was heading into an ambush.

It was when the machine plowed into the third field that the infuriated owners struck. A rain of stones, accurately hurled, fell on both crawler and driver. One crashed on the man's helmet. He gave a choked cry and half arose before he slumped forward limply over the controls. The machine ground on for a moment and then stopped, one tread tilted up against a boulder at an angle which threatened the stability of the whole vehicle.

Dane and Mura climbed down the side of the cliff. The driver might have deserved just what he had received. But he was human and they could not leave him to some alien vengeance. They could see nothing of the globes. But they took the precaution, when they had reached the valley floor, of spraying the bushes around the crawler with their sleep rays. Mura remained on guard, ready to supply a second dose of the harmless radiation while Dane ran forward to pull free the driver.

He lugged him back in a shoulder carry to the edge of the cliff where they could stand off an attack of the globes if necessary.

But either the sleep ray or the appearance on the scene of two more Terrans discouraged a second sortie. And the valley might well have been completely deserted as the two from the *Queen* stood ready, the limp body of the rescued at their feet.

"Shall we try it—" Dane nodded at the wall behind them. Mura contrived to look amused.

"Unless you are a crax seed chewer, I do not see how you are going to climb with our friend draped across your broad shoulders——"

Dane, now that it was called to his attention, could share that doubt. The cliff climbing act was one which required both hands and feet, and one could never do it with a dead weight to support.

The unconscious man groaned and moved feebly. Mura went down on one knee and studied the face framed by the dented helmet. First he unhooked the fellow's blaster belt and added it to his own armament. Then he loosened the chin strap, took off the battered headcovering and proceeded to slap the stubbled face dispassionately.

The crude resuscitation worked. Eyes blinked up at them and then the man tried to lever himself up, an operation Mura assisted with a jerk at his collar.

"It is time to go," the steward said. "This way——"

Together they got the man on his feet, and urged him along the wall, rounding the spur on which they had been perched all night, so coming to the hidden point where the other two of their party were camped.

The driver showed little interest in them, he was apparently concentrating on his uncertain balance. But Mura's grip was about his wrist and Dane guessed that that grasp was but the preliminary of one of the tricks of wrestling in which the steward was so well versed that no other of the *Queen*'s crew could defeat him.

As for Dane, he kept an eye behind, expecting any moment to be the target of a hail of those expertly thrown rocks. In a way this move they had just made would lead the Limbians to believe them one with the outlaws, and might well ruin any hopes they had cherished of establishing Trade relations with the queer creatures. And yet to leave a human at the mercy of the aliens was more than either of the Terrans could do.

Their charge spit a glob of blood and then spoke to Mura: "You one of the Omber crowd? I didn't know they'd been called in——"

Mura's expression did not change. "But this is a mission of importance, is it not? They have called many of us in——"

"Who beamed me back there? Those damned bogies?"

"The natives, yes. They threw stones——"

The man snarled. "We ought to roast 'em all! They hang around and try to crack our skulls every time we have to come through these hills. We'll have to use the blasters again—if we can catch up with 'em. Trouble is they move too fast——"

"Yes, they provide a problem," Mura returned soothingly. "Around here now——" He urged their captive around the point of the cliff into the other valley. But for the first time the man seemed to sense that something was wrong.

"Why go in here?" he asked, his pale eyes moving from one to the other of the Terrans. "This isn't a through valley."

"We have our crawler here. It would be better for you to ride—in your condition, would it not?" Mura continued persuasively.

"Huh? Yes, it might! I've a bad head, that's sure." His hand arose to his head and he winced as it touched a point above his right ear.

Dane let out his breath. Mura was running this perfectly. They were going to be able to get the fellow back where they wanted him without any trouble at all.

Mura had kept his clasp on their charge's arm, and now he steered him around a screen of boulders to face the crawler, Kosti and Wilcox. It was the machine that gave the truth away.

The captive stiffened and halted so suddenly that Dane bumped into him. His eyes shifted from the machine to the men by it. His hands went to his belt, only to tell him that he was unarmed.

"Who are you?" he demanded.

174

"That works two ways, fella," Kosti fronted him. "Suppose you tell us who *you* are——"

The man made as if to turn and looked over his shoulder down the valley as if hoping to see a rescue party there. Then Mura's grip screwed him back to his former position.

"Yes," the steward's soft voice added, "we greatly wish to know who you are."

The fact that he was fronted by only four must have triggered the prisoner's courage. "You're from the ship—" he announced triumphantly.

"We are from *a* ship," corrected Mura. "There are many ships on this world, many, many ships."

He might have slapped the fellow with his open hand, for the effect that speech had. And Dane was inspired to add:

"There is a Survey ship——"

The prisoner swayed, his bloodstained face pale under space tan, his lower lip pinched between his teeth as if by that painful gesture he could forego speech.

Wilcox had seated himself on the crawler. Now he calmly drew his blaster, balancing the ugly weapon on his knee pointing in the general direction of the prisoner's middle.

"Yes, there are quite a few ships here," he said. They might have been speaking of the weather, but for the set of the astrogator's jaw. "Which one do you think we hail from?"

But their captive was not yet beaten. "You're from the one out there—the *Solar Queen*."

"Why? Because no one survived in the others?"

Mura asked quietly. "You had better tell us what you know, my friend."

"That's right." Kosti moved forward a pace until his many inches loomed over the battered driver. "Save us time and you trouble, if you speak up now, flyboy. And the more time it takes, the more impatient we're going to get—understand?"

It was plain that the prisoner did. The threat which underlay Mura's voice was underlined by Kosti's reaching hands.

"Who are you and what are you doing here?" Wilcox began the interrogation for the second time.

The knockout delivered by the bogies had undoubtedly softened up the driver to begin with. But Dane was inclined to believe that it was Mura and Kosti who finished the process.

"I'm Lav Snall," he said sullenly. "And if you're from the *Solar Queen,* you know what I'm doing here. This isn't going to get you anywhere. We've got your ship grounded for just as long as we want."

"This is most interesting," Wilcox drawled. "So that ship out on the plain is grounded for as long as you want, is it? Where's your maul—invisible?"

The prisoner showed his teeth in a grin which was three quarters sneer. "We don't need a maul—not here on Limbo. This whole world's a trap—when we want to use it."

Wilcox spoke to Mura. "Was his head badly injured?"

The steward nodded. "It must have been—to addle his wits so. I can not judge truly, I am no medic."

Snall rose to the bait. "I'm not space-whirlly if

that's what you mean. You don't know what we found here—a Forerunner machine and it still operates! It can pull ships right out of space—bring 'em in here to crash. When that's running your *Queen* can't lift—not even if she were a Patrol Battlewagon, she couldn't. In fact we can pull in a battlewagon if and when we want to———!''

"Most enlightening," was Wilcox's comment. "So you've got some sort of an installation which can pull ships right out of space. That's a new one for me. Did the Whisperers tell you all about it?"

Snall's cheeks showed a tinge of dark red. "I'm not whirlly, I tell you!"

Kosti laid his hands on the prisoner's shoulders and forced him to sit down on a rock. "We know," he repeated in a mock soothing tone. "Sure—there's a great big machine here with a Forerunner running it. It reaches out and grabs—just like this!" He clutched with his own big fist at the empty air an inch or two beyond Snall's nose.

But the prisoner had recovered a little of his poise. "You don't have to believe me," he returned. "Just watch and see what happens if that pigheaded captain of yours tries to upship here. It won't be pretty. And it won't be long before you're gathered up, either———"

"I suppose you have ways of running us down?" Wilcox's left eyebrow slanted up under his helmet. "Well, you haven't contacted us yet and we've done quite a bit of traveling lately."

Snall looked from one to another. There was a faint puzzlement in his attitude.

"You're wearing Trade dress," he repeated aloud

the evidence gathered by his eyes. "You have to be from the *Queen*."

"But you're not quite sure, are you?" Mura prodded. "We may be from some other spacer you trapped with this Forerunner device. Are you certain that there are no other survivors of crashes roaming through these valleys?"

"If there are—they won't be walking about long!" was Snall's quick retort.

"No. You have your own way of dealing with them, don't you? With this?" Wilcox lifted the blaster so that it now centered upon the prisoner's head rather than his middle. "Just as you handled some of those aboard the *Rimbold*."

"I wasn't in on that!" Snall gabbled. In spite of the morning chill there were drops of moisture ringing his hairline.

"It seems to me that you are all outlaws," Wilcox continued, still in a polite, conversational tone. "Are you sure you haven't been Patrol Posted?"

That did it. Snall jumped. He got about a foot away before Kosti dragged him back.

"All right—so I've been posted!" he snarled at Wilcox as the jetman smacked him down on the rock once more. "What are you going to do about it? Burn me when I'm unarmed? Go ahead—do it!"

Traders could be ruthless, if the time and place demanded ice-cold tactics, but Dane knew now that the last thing Wilcox would do was to burn Snall down in cold blood. Even if the fact that he was Patrol Posted as a murderous criminal, with a price on his head, put him outside the law and absolved his killer from any future legal complications.

"Why should we kill you?" asked Mura calmly. "We are Free Traders. I think that you know very well what that means. A swift death by a blaster is a very easy way into the Greater Space, is it not? But out on the Rim, in the Wild Worlds, we have learned other tricks. So you do not believe that, Lav Snall?"

The steward had made no threatening grimaces, his pleasant face was as blandly cheerful as ever. But Snall's eyes jerked away from that face. He swallowed in a quick gulp.

"You wouldn't——" he began again, but there was no certainty in his protest. He must have realized that the competition he now faced was far more dangerous than he had estimated. There were tales about Free Traders, they were reputed to be as tough as the Patrol, and not nearly so bound by regulation. He believed that Mura meant exactly what he said.

"What do you want to know——"

"The truth," returned Wilcox.

"I've been giving it to you—straight," Snall protested. "We've found a Forerunner installation back in the mountains. It acts on ships—pulls them right out of space to crack up here after they move into the beam, or ray, or whatever it is. I don't know how it works. Nobody's even seen the thing except a few picked men who know something about com stuff——"

"Why didn't it act on the *Solar Queen* when she came in?" Kosti asked. "She landed perfectly."

"'Cause the thing wasn't turned on. You had Salzar on board, didn't you?"

"And who is Salzar?" it was Mura's turn to ask the question.

"Salzar—Gart Salzar. He was the first to see what a sweet thing we found here. He got us all under cover when Survey was snooping around. We lay low and Salzar knew that if this world was auctioned off we'd be in real trouble. He took a cruiser we'd patched up and beat the *Griswold* back to Naxos, and then contacted you. So we get a nice trader all empty and waiting to load our stuff——"

"Your loot? And how did *you* reach here—crash?"

"Salzar did ten—twelve years ago. He didn't make too bad a landing and he and those men of his who were still alive went snooping. They found the Forerunners' machine and studied it until they learned a bit about working it. Now they can switch it off when they want to. It was dead when Survey was prowling around here because Salzar was off planet and we were afraid we'd get him when he came in."

"A pity you didn't," Wilcox remarked. "And where is this machine?"

Snall shook his head. "I don't know." Kosti moved a step closer and Snall added swiftly, "That's the truth! Only Salzar's boys know where it is or how it works."

"How many of them?" Kosti asked.

"Salzar, and three, maybe four others. It's back in the mountains—there somewhere——" He stabbed a finger, a shaking finger, in the general direction of the range.

"I think you can do better than that," Kosti was beginning when Dane cut in:

"What was Snall doing driving that crawler in here—if he didn't know where he was going?"

Mura's eyelids dropped as he adjusted the buckle of his helmet. "I think we have been slightly remiss. We should have a sentry aloft. There may be one of Snall's friends along."

Snall studiously studied the toes of his boots. Dane went to the cliff.

"I'll take a look-see," he offered.

To his first sight the situation on the plain had not changed. The *Queen*, all hatches sealed, rested just as she had at twilight the night before. With his glasses he could make out the small encampments of outlaws. But close to his own post he saw something else.

One of the strange crawlers had pulled away from the nearest camp. Seated behind the driver were two others and between them a fourth passenger, his brown Trade tunic not to be mistaken.

"Rip!" Though Dane could not see that prisoner's face he was sure the captive was Shannon. And the crawler was headed toward the valley where the bogies had ambushed the first!

Now was their chance to not only rescue Rip but make a bigger gap in the besiegers' force. Dane crawled to the edge of the cliff and, not daring to call, waved vigorously to attract the attention of those below. Mura and Wilcox nodded and Kosti headed the prisoner into greater seclusion. Then Dane sought a vantage point and waited with rising excitement for the enemy crawler to enter the valley.

14   TRUMPET OF JERICHO

"IT IS TIME, I believe," Mura had come up on the lookout point, "to follow the tactics of our fellow fighters, these 'bogies.' How is your throwing arm, Thorson?" He stooped and searched the ground, rising a few moments later grasping a round stone about as big as his fist.

Taking aim he pitched it at an angle into the valley and they saw and heard it strike against a rock there. Dane saw the reason for such an attack upon the crawler. Blaster fire was no respecter of persons. In an exchange of such potent forces Rip might well be killed or maimed. But rocks expertly thrown from above would not only knock out the outlaws, but would suggest an attack by native Limbians and not betray the identity of the attackers.

Kosti circled around the foot of the cliff and took cover below the perch favored by Mura, while Dane skimmed across the valley and climbed above eye level to a narrow ledge on which he might crouch with a pile of hastily collected ammunition.

They were not given long for such preparations, the clinking passage of the crawler echoed ahead as a

182

warning and the three Traders took to cover as the vehicle crept into sight across the uneven terrain. It crashed through bushes until the driver slowed to a halt. His helmet com-unit must have been on, for, while his natural voice could only have been an undistinguishable murmur to those in hiding, his words were loud in their ears.

"There's Snall's wagon—piled up! What's been——?"

One of Rip's guards scrambled off the crawler as if to go forward and investigate. And in that moment Mura's arm signaled Dane to attack.

A stone thudded against the helmet of the would-be investigator, sending him off balance to clutch at the tread of the crawler for support. Dane slammed another in his direction and then aimed for the driver of the machine.

They were yelling now and Rip had come to life. Though his arms were tied behind him, he threw himself at the man to his left, his effort carrying them both to the ground beyond. The driver turned on the power of the crawler so that it ground ahead through the rain of stones the three Traders hurled at it.

One of the outlaws had pulled himself aboard again and now the other wriggled from under Rip's body. He had his blaster in hand and he bent over Shannon with an evil grin. Then his face was smashed into a red pulp. He screamed horribly and reeled back. The one who had managed to climb aboard looked back in time to witness his fall.

"Kraner—those little beasts got Kraner! No, don't wait to collect that Trader! If you do they'll get us!"

The crawler kept on toward the mountains. For some reason the two on board it had not used their blasters to rake the bushes. The very unexpectedness of the attack and the loss of one of their company left them only with the thought of escape.

They rounded the length of the stranded crawler and were out of sight before Kosti crept out of hiding and went down to Rip, where Dane joined him seconds later.

Shannon lay on his side, his arms bound at a painful angle behind him, his face showing a closed eye surrounded with a dark bruise, a cut lip, raw and bloody.

"You *have* been to the wars," Kosti grunted as he knelt to saw at the cords with his bush knife.

Rip's words were mumbled as he tried to move his torn mouth. "They jumped me—I was almost to the *Queen* when they jumped me. They've the ship pinned here—some sort of ray which crashes any ship within a certain distance of the planet——"

Dane slipped an arm under Rip's shoulders and helped him to sit up. The other gave a grunt and a muffled exclamation as he moved, one hand going to his side.

"More damages?" Kosti reached out to unseal Rip's tunic but Shannon parried the investigating hand.

"Nothing we can fix here and now. Think I've cracked a rib—or maybe two. But, listen, they've the *Queen*——"

"We know. Picked up a prisoner," Dane told him. "He was driving that crawler over there. Told us all about what's going on here. Maybe, using him, we can make some sort of a deal. Can you walk——?''

''Yes, it might be well to withdraw.'' Mura stepped down to where they were. They had their coms on when we jumped them. It is uncertain how much of the succeeding events have been overheard by their fellows.''

Rip could walk, with support. And they got him around to their own crawler and Wilcox.

''Any sign of Kamil?'' Kosti wanted to know.

''They have him all right,'' Rip replied. ''But I think that he's with their main party. They have quite a few men. And they can keep the *Queen* here until she rusts away—if they want to.''

''So Snall here has already informed us,'' Wilcox observed bleakly. ''He also says that he does not know where this mysterious installation is. I'm inclined to doubt that——''

At that the bound and gagged prisoner wriggled and made muffled sounds, trying to indicate his sincerity.

''Down that valley is one way in, at least in to their major supply depot and barracks,'' Rip informed them. ''And the installation can't be too far from that.''

Dane touched the wriggling Snall with the toe of his boot. ''D'you suppose we could exchange this one for Ali? Or at least use him to get us into the place?''

Rip answered that. ''I doubt it. They're a pretty hard lot. Snall's life or death wouldn't matter much as far as they are concerned.''

And the look in those bloodshot eyes above the

gag Kosti had planted, bore out that Snall agreed with that. He had little faith in assistance from his own companions unless his rescue was necessary to their preservation.

"Three of us on our feet and able to go, and two crooks," Wilcox mused. "How many men have they back in the mountains, Shannon, any idea of that?"

"Maybe a hundred. It seems to be a well or-ganized outfit," Rip replied dispiritedly.

"We can sit here until we starve," Kosti broke the ensuing silence, "and that won't get us anywhere, will it? I'd say take some chances and hope for luck. It can't all be bad!"

"Snall could show us the way in—at least into the part he knows," Dane said. "And we could scout around—size up the country and the odds."

"If we could only contact the *Queen!*" Wilcox beat his knee with his fist.

"With the sun up—it is now—there is perhaps a way," Mura began.

His way entailed going back to the wrecked crawler in the second valley, and unscrewing a bright metal plate which backed the driver's seat. With Dane's help, the steward got this to the top of the cliff. And they wedged their prize at an angle until they caught the sun on its surface and flashed the light across the mile or so of rugged territory which lay between them and the ship.

Mura smiled. "This may do it. It should be as good as our torches in the night if it works. And unless those outlaws down there have eyes in the back of their skulls, it will not be seen except from control———''

But once their crude com was in place they had other preparations to make. Wilcox, Rip, Kosti and the prisoner moved from the hideout in one valley on into the other. The strange crawler was righted and found to be undamaged and ready to move. And while the other four waited Mura and Dane climbed once more to the heights where they sweated over the plate until they laboriously flashed twice over their message to the *Queen*.

Then there was nothing to do but stay to see if their code had been read. Only if the ship made the proper reply in action could they move.

And that answer came just as Dane had given up hope. Round ports blinked like eyes on the sides of the *Queen!* There was a bark of sound and smoke arose by a hidden pocket of besiegers—the one which lay between the ship and the valley. Their message had been read, those on the ship would keep the enemy bracketed while the party in the valley made their dash for the outlaw headquarters on a desperate attempt at surprise.

They were all able to ride on this carrier, the prisoner sandwiched in between Dane and Mura, Kosti at the controls. It had what their own crawler had lacked, handholds, and they clung to these as the thing rattled along.

Dane watched the bushy slopes they passed. He had not forgotten the bogie attack. It might be true that the creatures were nocturnal. But on the other hand, once aroused, perhaps the globes might still be in hiding there, waiting to cut off any small party.

The valley curved and narrowed. Now under the jolting carrier the surface was mostly stream bed and the water crept up to lap at the edge of the platform. There were signs here, as there had been in the valley near the ruins, that this way had been in use as a road—scratches on the rocks, tracks crushed in the gravel.

Then before them the stream became a small falls, splashing into a pool and the valley ended in a barrier cliff. Kosti jerked the gag from Snall's mouth.

"All right," he said in the tone of one who was not to be put off, "what do we do to get through here, bright boy?"

Snall licked his puffed lips and glowered back. Bound and gagged as he had been, helpless as he was, he had regained a large measure of his confidence.

"Find out for yourself," he retorted.

Kosti sighed. "I hate to waste time, fella. But if you must be softened up, you're going to be—get me?"

Something else got them all first. A stone missed Kosti's head by a scant inch as he bent over Snall. And a larger one struck the captive's body, bringing a sharp cry of pain out of him.

"Bogies!" Dane fanned his sleep ray up a wall where he could see nothing move, but from which he was sure the stones had been thrown.

Another rock cracked viciously against the crawler as Wilcox hit dirt on the other side, pulling Rip with him to shelter half under the machine. Mura was using his ray, too, standing unconcerned knee deep in the pool and beaming the cliff foot by foot as if he had all the time in the world and intended to make this a thorough job.

It was Snall who ended that strange blind battle. Kosti had dragged him to safety and must have cut his bonds so that he could move with greater speed. But now the outlaw flung himself out of shelter, straight for the controls of the carrier. He brought his fist down upon a button set in the panel and was rewarded by a high pitched tinkle—a tinkle which resounded in the Terrans' heads until Dane had to fight to keep his hands from his ears.

The answer to this assault upon their eardrums was as preposterous as anything Dane had ever witnessed in a Video performance. The supposedly solid rock wall fronting the end of the valley opened, one piece of the stone falling back to provide a dark gap. And, since their captive was prepared for that he was the first through the door, darting from under Kosti's clutching hands.

With an inarticulate roar the jetman followed Snall. And Dane pounded after both of them into the maw of the cliff. From the sunlight of Limbo they were translated to a twilight gray, strung out like beads on a string, with Snall, proving himself a good distance runner, well at the head.

Dane was inside the straight corridor before his common sense took command once more. He shouted to Kosti and his voice echoed in a hollow boom. Though he slowed, the other two kept on into the dusky reaches ahead.

Dane turned back to the entrance, still undecided. To be cut off here—their party divided. What should he do, run after Kosti, or try to bring in the others? He was in time to see Mura come in at a walking pace. And then, to Dane's horror, the outlet to the world closed! There was a clang of metal meeting metal and the sunlight was instantly cut to evening.

"The door!" Dane hurled himself at the masked opening with the same fervor with which he had followed Snall into the corridor. But before he reached that spot Mura's steadying grip closed on his arm, restraining him with a strength he had forgotten the smaller man possessed.

"Do not be alarmed," the steward said. "There is no danger. Wilcox and Shannon are in safety. They are armed with the sleep rays, in addition they know how to operate the horn to open the gate when necessary. But where is Karl? Has he disappeared?"

Mura's tone had a soothing effect. The litle man gave such an impression of unruffled efficiency that Dane lost that panic which had sent him running for the entrance.

"The last I saw he was still after Snall."

"Let us hope that he has caught up with him. I would be better pleased if we walked these ways with Snall under our control—not with him some-where ahead to warn his companions."

They hurried on and discovered that the corridor made a sharp turn to the left. Dane listened, hoping to hear the sounds of running feet. But when the thump-thump did come it was made by a single pair of boots. And a minute later the jetman barged into view, his face very sober in the wan light radiated from the smooth walls about them.

"Where's Snall?" Dane asked.

Kosti grimaced. "He got through one of those condemned walls back there——"

"Just where?" Mura went in the direction from which the jetman had just come.

"The door snapped shut as I got to it," Kosti protested. "We can't follow him. Unless one of you brought that tootler off the crawler."

The passage stretched only a short distance beyond, ending in a wall as blank of any opening as the cliffs without. Though this was not of stone but of the seamless substance which made the buildings in the Forerunner ruins.

"This wall?" Mura thumped the surface as Kosti nodded gloomily.

"Can't see any opening there now——"

The humming vibration, to which they had become so accustomed that they no longer consciously noted it, sang through the walls, through the flooring under their feet. How much that sonic resonance added to their feeling of uneasiness it was hard to tell. But the narrow corridor, the pallid light, fed their sensation of being trapped.

"Looks as if we are stuck," the jetman observed, "unless we go out into the valley again. How about that? Where's Wilcox and Shannon?"

Dane explained. But he, too, hoped that the others would use the horn and open the outer door. With the intention of getting back to the entrance he walked along the hall. That passage had run straight, he remembered, and then there had been a right angle turn around which Kosti had disappeared in pursuit of Snall——

But when Dane came to that corner and made the

turn he was fronted not by the hall he remembered, but a pocket of some three or four feet. He stopped, bewildered. There had been only one corridor—with no openings along its sides. Before him now should be a smooth stretch leading to the outer door. But instead here was another wall. He reached out and his nails scraped on its slick surface. It was there all right—no illusion.

A muffled cry brought him about and he was just in time to see another barrier appear out of the side wall to seal off a second segment of the passage, one to cut him away from the others.

Dane threw himself forward, barely getting through the narrowing space. And he might not have made it had Kosti not come to his aid and used his bull's strength to wrestle against the sliding wall. But as Dane won to the other side, it clicked triumphantly into place and they were boxed in a six foot section of corridor.

"Neat," Kosti commented. "Got us shut up until they have time to attend to us."

Mura shrugged. "It can not now be doubted that Snall got through with his alarm."

But the steward did not appear bothered. Kosti thumped the wall, listening intently as if he hoped to discover the trick of its opening by the sound he so invoked.

"Remote control, of course," Mura continued in his placid tone. "Yes, they will now believe that they have us safe——"

"Only they don't do they?" Observance of Mura led Dane to that question.

"That we shall see. The outer door is controlled

by sonics. I heard Tang say that the installation interference lies partly in the non-audible range. So it may be we have an answer to this trap.''

He unsealed the front of his tunic and groped in the inner breast pocket all Traders used for their most prized possessions. He took out a three inch tube of polished white substance which might have been bone.

Kosti stopped his thumping. ''Say—that's your Feedle call——''

''Just so. Now we shall see if it can be used for another purpose than to summon the insects of Karmuli——''

He put the miniature pipe to his lips and blew though no sound issued to be caught by Terran hearing. Kosti's shade of elation vanished.

''No use——''

Mura smiled. ''You have no patience, Karl. This has ten ultrasonic notes. I have only used one. Give me a chance to try the others before you are sure we do not possess a key to these doors.''

There followed long moments of silence with no visible result.

''Not going to work——'' Kosti shook his head.

But Mura paid no attention. At intervals he took the pipe from his lips, rested, and then tried again. Dane was certain that he must have tried more than ten notes, but the steward showed no sign of discouragement.

''That's more than ten notes,'' accused Kosti.

''The signal that opened the first door employed three. The same number combination may apply here.'' He raised the pipe once more.

Kosti sat down on the floor, obviously divorcing himself from proceedings he deemed useless. Dane squatted beside him. But Mura's patience was infinite. One hour passed—by Dane's watch, and they were well into the second. Dane wondered about their air supply. Unless it oozed through the walls as did the light, he could see no way in which it was renewed. And yet that about them was fresh.

"That tootling," Kosti sounded fretful, "isn't going to do any good. You'll wear the pipe out before you get through this—" he struck his hand against the side wall.

And under his touch the section of wall moved, showing a dark crack a couple of inches wide extending from the floor to a point six feet up.

15   PRISONER'S MAZE

"YOU'VE DONE IT!" Dane cried to Mura as Kosti tore at the opening, forcing it larger—the door resisting as if it had not moved for a long time.

"This isn't the right way," the jetman protested even as he pushed.

"Not the corridor, no," agreed Mura. "But this *is* a way out of our present trap and as such it is not to be despised. Also it is not one in general use, or so I would judge by its stubbornness. Therefore, an even better path for us. I must have hit upon a rarer sonic combination—" He wiped the tiny pipe carefully and put it away.

Though Kosti forced the door open as wide as it would go, the resulting entrance was a narrow one. Mura negotiated it without trouble, but Dane and the jetman had to squeeze. And for one dangerous moment it seemed that the latter might not be able to make it. Only by shedding his bulky equipment belt and his outdoor tunic could he scrape by.

They found themselves in a second corridor, one more narrow than that in which they had been imprisoned. The same gray light glowed from the walls. But as Dane stepped forward his feet were cushioned and he looked down to see that his boots stirred fine dust, dust thick enough to coat the floor an inch or more in depth.

Mura freed his belt torch and sent its beam ahead. Save where they had disturbed it, that dust was smooth, without track. No one had walked this way for a long, long time—perhaps not since the Forerunners had left this mountain citadel.

"Hey!" Kosti's startled cry drew their attention. Where the narrow door had been was now once more smooth wall. Their retreat had been cut off.

"They've trapped us again!" he added hoarsely. But Mura shook his head.

"I think not. There is perhaps some closing mechanism that operates automatically, which we activated merely by passing it. No one uses this passage—or hasn't for years. I am willing to believe that Rich and the others do not even know of its existence. Let us see where it will lead us." He pattered ahead eagerly.

The corridor paralleled for a space that wider hall which had been turned into a trap. Its smooth walls showed no other hint of openings. There might be innumerable doors along it, all attuned to some combination of whistled notes, Dane thought, but they had neither the time nor the energy to explore that possibility.

"Air——"

Dane did not need that exclamation from Mura—he had already scented it. Cutting across the dusty, dead atmosphere of the way was a breath of stronger air—a puff which carried with it the chill of the outer world, and a very faint hint of growing stuff which out in the open might not have been discernible at all.

The three reached the point from which that came, and found an opening in the wall. Beyond, audible above the beat of the installation, was a rushing sound. Dane thrust his hand out into the square of dark and the current of air, blowing as if sucked in by the mountain, pulled gently at his fingers.

"Ventilation system," Kosti's engineering knowledge was intrigued. He put head and shoulders into the opening. "Big enough to travel through," he reported after using his torch up and down the channel beyond.

"Something to keep in mind," Mura agreed. "But first let us get to the end of this particular way."

In twenty minutes they got to the end, another blank wall. Kosti was not disheartened this time.

"Bring out the tootler, Frank," was his solution, "and open her up for us———"

But Mura did not reach for the pipe. Instead he swept his torch carefully over the wall. This was not the smooth material of the Forerunners' work, but the rough native stone of the mountain.

"I do not think that this will respond to any toot-ling," he remarked. "This is the end of the road and it is truly sealed———"

"But a passage should lead somewhere!" Dane protested.

"Yes. Undoubtedly there are many openings we can not see. And we do not know the sonic combina-tions to unlock them. I do not think it wise to waste time trying to find any such. Let us return to that air duct. If it supplies a series of passages it may let us out into another one——''

So they went back to the duct. As Kosti had said, it was large, large enough that the jetman and Dane might travel it—if they went on hands and knees. And it lacked the dust which carpeted the side passage.

One after another they swung into it, and into the dark as they moved from the entrance. For here was none of the ghostly radiance which gave limited light to the corridors.

Mura crawled first, his torch beaming on. They were in a tube of generous proportions, and around them passed air which had come from the outside. But the steady beat of the installation crept up their arms and legs from contact with the surface.

The steward switched off his torch. ''Light ahead——'' his voice was no more than a husky whisper.

When Dane's eyes adjusted to the lack of torchlight he saw it too—a round circle of pale gray. They had found the end of the vent.

But as they came up to that exit they found themselves fronted by a grille of metal, a mesh wide enough to allow passage of their hands through the squares. And beyond it lay a vast open space. Mura looked through and for the first time since he had known him Dane heard the unusually calm steward give a gasp of real surprise. Dane prodded his back suggesting that he and Kosti also wanted to see.

Mura flattened himself against the wall of the tube so that Dane could take his place. The space beyond was huge—as if the whole of a mountain interior had been hollowed out to hold a most curious structure. For, when the cargo-apprentice squirmed forward he looked down upon the strangest building he had ever seen.

It was roofless, its outer walls coming up to within six feet of the ventilation grille. But those walls—they ran crazily at curves and angles, marking off irregular spaces which bore small resemblances to ordinary rooms. Corridors began nowhere and ended in six, or eight-sided chambers without other exit. Or a whole series of rooms were linked—for no purpose since the end ones possessed neither entrance nor exit.

The walls were thick, at least three feet wide. A man could swing down and walk along them, so discovering the purpose of the muddled maze, or winning completely across the cave. And since there was no way back for them, that is what the Terrans must do. Dane inched back to allow Kosti his turn at the grille.

With a grunt of surprise the jetman viewed the weird scene. "What's it for?" he wanted to know. "It doesn't make sense——"

"Maybe not our brand of sense, no," Mura agreed. "But the solidity of the work suggests a very definite purpose. No one builds such erections for a mere whim."

Dane reached over Kosti's shoulder to pull at the grille. "We'll have to get through this——"

"Yes, and then what?" the jetman wanted to know. "Do we grow wings?"

"We can get down to the top of that wall. They're wide enough to walk on. So we can get across on them———"

Kosti was very quiet. Then his big hands went out to the grille, testing the fastenings. "Take a while to get this loose." From his belt he took his small tool kit and busied himself about the frame of the netting.

They ate while they crouched there, rations from their emergency kits. Since the gray light of the cave neither waxed nor waned, there was no measurement of time saved as recorded on their watches. It might have been the middle of the night—their time keepers said it was afternoon.

Kosti gulped his vita-cube and went back to work on the grille. It was well into the second hour before he put away his tools.

"Now!" he pushed gently at the grille and it folded out, leaving the end of the tube open. But he did not swing through as Dane expected. Instead he crawled back and allowed the others to pass him. Mura thrust his head through the opening and then looked back at Dane.

"I shall have to have help to reach the wall. I am too short———"

He held out his hands and Dane clamped a hold about his wrists. Mura backed cautiously out of the vent and for a moment his weight pulled Dane forward. In that same instant the younger man felt Kosti's grip about his hips giving him the anchorage he needed as he lowered the steward to the wall.

"Made it!" Mura trotted several feet to the right on the wall and stood waiting.

Dane turned to lower himself to the same level.

"Good luck!" Kosti said out of the shadows. Instead of crouching ready to follow, the jetman had moved back in the tube.

"What do you mean?" Dane asked, chilled by something in the other's attitude.

"You've got to go this next stretch by yourselves, fella," Kosti returned calmly enough. "I haven't any head for heights. I can't balance along on those walls down there—two steps and I'd be over the edge."

Dane had forgotten the big man's disability. But what were they going to do? The only way out of here lay across the maze of walls, a maze Kosti could not tread. On the other hand, they could not leave the jetman here.

"Listen, boy," Kosti continued. "You two will have to go on. I'll stay right here. If there is a way out and you find it, well, then maybe I can make it. But, until you are sure, there's no use in my going along to foul you up. That's only good sense——"

Maybe it was good sense, but Dane could not accept it. However, a moment later he had no chance to protest. Kosti's hands were iron about his wrists, the jetman pushed him to the edge of the duct and thrust him through, dangling him until his boots scraped the wall. Then Kosti let go.

"Kosti won't come— He says he can't make it!"

Mura nodded. "To walk these——" he indicated the maze of walls, "would be impossible for him now. But if we can find a way out—then we can return and guide him. We will move faster alone, and Karl knows that——"

Still feeling as if he were deserting Kosti, Dane

reluctantly followed the steward who picked a cat's surefooted way along the wall out into the scrambled pattern beyond. The walls were about twenty feet high and the rooms and corridors they formed were bare of any furnishings. There were no signs that anyone had been there for centuries. That is, there were not, until Mura gave a sudden exclamation and aimed the beam of his torch down into a narrow room.

Dane crowded up beside him to see it, too, a tangle of white bones, a skull staring hollow-eyed back at them. The maze had had an inhabitant once, one who remained for eternity.

Mura swung the beam in slow circles about the skeleton. There were some dark rags of clothing, and the light glimmered back at them from a buckle of untarnished metal.

"A prisoner," said the steward slowly. "A man shut into this could wander perhaps forever and never find his way out——"

"You mean that he has been here since—since —" Dane could not name the stretch of time which had elapsed since the destruction of the city, the burn-off of Limbo.

"I think not. This one, he was human—like us. He has been here a long time certainly, but not so long as it has been since the builders left this maze. Others have found it, and a use for so puzzling a structure."

Now as they went from one wall to the next, twisting and turning, but always aiming at the center of the maze, they kept careful watch for other remains in the sections below. The whole space filled with this curious honeycomb erection was much larger, Dane came to realize, than it had appeared from the air duct. There must be several square miles of plain solid walls crossing, curving, and criss-crossing to shut in nothing but oddly shaped emptiness.

"For a reason," Mura murmured. "This must have a purpose, been made for a reason—but why? The geometry is wrong—as were the lines of the buildings in the city. This is Forerunner work. But why—why should they contrive such a thing?"

"For a prison?" Dane suggested. "Put someone in here and they would never get out. Prison and execution chamber in one."

"No," Mura shook his head. "It is too large an undertaking—men do not go to such lengths to handle their criminals. There are shorter and less arduous methods for imposing justice."

"But the Forerunners may not have been 'men.' "

"Not our kind of 'men,' perhaps. But what do we mean by the word 'man'? We use it loosely to mean an intelligent being, able in part to rule both his environment and his destiny. Surely the Forerunners were 'men' by those tests. But you can not lead me to think that they meant this merely as a prison and place of execution!"

In spite of the fact that they were both surefooted and had a head for heights, neither hurried on these high narrow ways. Dane discovered that to stare too much at the passages and the rooms had an odd effect on his sense of balance and it was necessary to pause now and then and gaze up into the neutral gray overhead in order to settle an uneasy stomach. And all the while through the walls there arose the beat of the mighty machine which must be housed somewhere within the mountain range of which this maze could be a not insignificant part. As Mura had pointed out the geometry of the place was "wrong" in Terran sight, it produced in the Traders a sensation which bordered on fear.

They found the second dead man well beyond the first. And this time their light picked out a tunic with insignia they knew—a Survey man.

"It may not have been built for a prison," Dane commented, "but they must be using it for one now."

"This one has been dead for months," Mura kept his light trained on the huddled body. But Dane refused to look again. "He may have been from the *Rimbold*—or from some other lost ship."

"They could have bagged more than one Survey ship with that infernal machine of theirs. I'll wager there're a good lot of wrecks lying about."

"That is the truth." Mura arose from his knees. "And for this poor one we can do no good. Let us go——"

Only too eager to get away from that mute evidence of an old tragedy, Dane started on, moving from one wall to the corner of an adjoining one.

"Wait—!" The steward raided his hand as well as his voice in that emphatic order.

Obediently Dane halted. The steward's whole stance expressed listening. Then Dane too caught that sound, the ring of boots on stone, space boots with their magnetic sole plates clicking in an irregular rhythm as if the wearer was reeling as he ran.

Mura listened, then he took a quick turn to the right and headed back in the general direction from which they had just come.

The sound died away and Mura quested about like a hunting hound, making short assays right and left, shining his torch into one narrow, angled compartment after another.

He was stopping above a section of corridor which ran reasonably straight when the click of those steps began again. But this time they were slower, with intervals between, as if the runner was almost at the end of his strength. Some other poor devil was trapped in here—if they could only find him! Dane pushed on as avidly as Mura.

But in here sound was a tricky guide. The walls echoed, muffled or broadcast it, so that they could not be sure of anything but the general direction. They worked their way along, about two sections apart, flashing the light into each cornered room.

Dane followed his narrow footing halfway around a room which had six walls, each of a different length, and transferred to the top of one which was part of a curving hallway. Then he sighted movement at one of those curves, a figure who lurched forward, one hand on the wall for support.

"Over here!" he called to the steward.

The man below had come to the end of that hall— another wall—and as he half fell against the obstruction and slipped to the floor he groaned. Then he lay motionless, face down, twenty feet below his would-be rescuer. And Dane, eyeing that perfectly smooth expanse, did not see how they could get down to offer aid.

Mura ran lightly up the narrow footpaths as if he had spent all his life traveling maze walls. His circle of light touched Dane's as they spotlighted the body.

There was no mistaking the ripped tunic of their Service. The captive was a trader—one of their own. They did not know whether he was aware of their torches, but suddenly he moaned and rolled over on his back, exposing a face cut and bruised, the result of a skillful and brutal beating. Dane might now have been able to recognize him but Mura was certain.

"Ali!"

Perhaps Kamil heard that, or perhaps it was just his steel will which roused him. He moaned again and then uttered some undistinguishable words through torn lips as his puffed and swollen eyes turned up toward them.

"Ali—" Mura called. "We are here. Can you attend—do you understand?"

Kamil's blackened face was up, he forced out coherent words. "Who—? Can't see!"

"Mura, Thorson," the steward identified them crisply. "You are hurt?"

"Can't see. Lost—Hungry——"

"How are we going to get down?" Dane wanted to know. If they only had the ropes which had linked them to the crawler in the fog! But those were behind and here were no substitutes.

Mura unhooked his belt. "Your belt and mine——"

"They aren't long enough, even together!"

"No, not in themselves, but we shall see—"

Dane shed his belt and watched the steward buckle

it end to end with his own. Then the smaller man spoke to Thorson.

"You must lower me. Can you do it?"

Dane looked about doubtfully. The wall top was smooth and bare of anything in the way of an anchor. If he couldn't take the weight of the steward he would be jerked over and they would both fall. But there was no other way.

"Do my best—" He lay belly down on the wall, hooking the toes of his boots on either side and thrusting his left arm out and down into the neighboring room. Mura had drawn his blaster and was making careful adjustments to its barrel.

"Here I go—" With the blaster in one hand the steward swung over, his other fist twisted in the rope of linked belts. Dane held on grimly in spite of the tearing wrench in his shoulder.

He blinked and ducked his head at a sudden flash of burning fire. The fumes of blaster fire assaulted his throat and nose and he understood at last what Mura was attempting. The steward was burning out hand and foot holds in the smooth surface of the wall as he descended, cutting a ladder to reach Ali.

16   THE HEART OF LIMBO

ALL AT ONCE Mura's weight was gone, the strain on his shoulders no longer pulled him apart. Dane looked over the edge of the wall. A series of holes, black near him, still glowing red farther down, were clear to see in the gloom. His aching fingers released hold on the belts and they clattered to the floor.

When the red faded from the last of the holes the blaster had cut, Dane pulled on the gloves, clipped to his tunic cuffs against the cold of Limbo, and swung over to test the ladder. Though it ended well above the floor, he dropped the last few feet without difficulty.

Mura had out his aid kit and was working on Ali's beaten face as Dane came up.

"The torch," the steward ordered impatiently, "give me some light here!"

So Dane provided the light needed for the job of temporary patchwork. When the steward was done, Ali was able to see a little and had beeen supplied with a vita-cube and a limited drink of emergency stimulant. He could not twist his battered features with a smile, but some of the old light tone was back in his voice as he spoke:

"How did you get here—by flitter?"

Mura got to his feet and gazed up into the vast dome which arched above the maze.

"No. But one could be of use here, yes——"

"Yes is right!" Torn and swollen lips kept Kamil's words a mumble, but the engineer-apprentice was determined to talk. "I thought I was coasting with dead jets all right until you showed up. When that Rich shut me in here he said there was a way out if I were just clever enough to find it. But I didn't think it meant you had to have wings!"

"What is this anyway?" Dane asked. "Their prison?"

"Partly that, partly something else. You know what's going on here?" Ali's voice was shrill with excitement. "They've found an installation left by the Forerunners—and the thing still runs! It brings down any ship within a certain range—smash 'em up here. Then this gang of Patrol Posteds goes out and loots the wrecks!"

"They've got the *Queen* pinned down," Dane told him. "If she tries to lift she'll crash——"

"So that's it! They have had to run the machine at a more steady pace than usual and there was some talk—before they threw me in here—about how long it will go without a rest. Seems that before it switched on and off mechanically after some impulse pattern they don't understand. Anyway, the key to the whole set-up is somewhere here in this blasted puzzle house!"

"The installation is here?" Mura eyed the walls about them as if he were ready to pull the secret out of their very substance.

"Either that, or something important concerning it. There is a way through here—if you know the trail. Twice since I've been wandering around I heard people talking, once just on the other side of a wall. Only I never could get through to the right halls—" Ali sighed. "I had about reached the end of my orbit when you came jetting out of the ether."

Dane buckled his belt around him and now he drew his blaster. With it on the lowest pressure he began to use it, methodically burning a series of holds to meet those Mura had left at a higher level.

"We can go and see," he said as he worked.

"You will go," Mura told him. "And you will do it with secrecy—avoiding as much as possible any trouble. Ali can not walk the walls, not now. But see if from above you can find this trail he talks of. Then with your guidance we can move——"

That was sensible enough. Dane waited for the pocks to cool, listening to Mura explain all that had happened since Ali had disappeared, hearing in turn Kamil's account of his own adventures.

"There were two of them waiting in ambush and they jumped me," he said with open disgust at his own lack of caution. "They had individual flyers!" There was awe in his tone. "Something else they found here. Great Space, this place is a storehouse of Forerunner material! Rich is using things he doesn't know the meaning of—or why they work—or anything! These mountains are a regular warehouse. Well, with those flyers on they nipped me up and out—knocked me out. And when I came to I was tied up on one of those worm crawlers of theirs. Then I had a little question session with Rich and a couple of his burn-off boys——'' Ali's voice sounded grim and he did not go into details, his face gave evidence enough of that period. ''Afterwards they made a few bright remarks and shoved me in here and I've probably been going around in circles ever since. But—do you realize—this place, it's what everyone had been hunting for for years! Forerunner material—good as the day it was made. If we can get out of here——''

''Yes, first the getting out,'' Mura cut in. ''Also the matter of the installation——''

Dane glanced at the top of the wall. ''How am I going to find you here again?''

''You will take bearings. Also,'' Mura brought out his torch, set it up on end and snapped the low power button. ''When you are aloft, see what kind of guide this makes——''

Once more Dane made use of the holds and scrambled up on the wall. He looked back. Yes, the beam from the torch cut straight up in the gloom. In a very inferior way it was not unlike the beacon on the *Queen*. He waved his hand to the two below and started out, heading for the center of the maze where Ali believed the secret of the installation lay.

Walls angled, curved, took him right or left, so he had to retrace time and again. And nowhere did he see any hall below which led through the puzzle without interruption. If there was such a one, its doorways might be controlled by sonics and so hidden to the casual search.

But through his body coursed the heavy beat of the hidden machine. He must be nearing the source. Then he was conscious of a heightened glow in the grayness ahead. It had none of the sharp quality of a torch ray—rather it was as if the spectral radiance of the walls had been stepped to a more concentrated degree in that section. He slowed his pace to a shuffle as he neared that center, afraid that the click of his metallic boot plates might betray him.

What he came to first was a double wall forming an oval area, a space of three feet between the two smooth surfaces. Determined to see what lay within, he made a risky jump from one to the next and then crouched on his hands and knees, creeping up to peer down into a room which was in stark contrast to the territory about it.

There were machines here—huge towering things—each sealed into a box coating. And a good third of the encircling wall was a bank of controls and dials, centered by a wide plate of smooth metal which bore a likeness to the visaplates he knew.

But that screen mirrored no scene from the outer world on its surface. Instead it was uniformly black and across it moved sparks of light.

Watching this were three men. And, by the brighter light, Dane was able to recognize Salzar Rich as well as the Rigellian who had come in on the *Queen*. The third man, in a seat just before the screen, his hands resting on a wide keyboard, was one he had never seen before.

This was it! This was the rotten heart of Limbo which rendered the blasted planet a menace to her particular corner of space! And as long as that heart beat, as it was doing now in waves which he could feel through his whole body, the *Queen* was tied to danger and her crew were helpless——

But were they? Dane felt a tiny thrill of excitement. Rich was making use of machines he did not really understand. And under other hands the whole set-up could be rendered harmless. Perhaps by watching now he himself could discover how to control the broadcast which kept the *Queen* a prisoner.

The points of light moved on the screen and the three men watched with a concentration of interest which argued of some anxiety. None of them made any move to touch the levers or buttons on the panel. Dane wriggled on his belly toward a point from which he could overhear any orders Rich might give.

So he was flattened out of sight a few minutes later when the sound of running feet startled him. Someone was coming through the maze. It was one of the outlaws and he wove a path from crooked hall to angled room in a manner which proved that he knew the secret. As he came up against the barrier he threw back his head and shouted, his voice ringing in the vast dome over their heads:

"Salzar!"

Rich whirled and then he flung out his right hand and made some adjustment on the panel. A section of the wall slid back to admit the newcomer.

Rich's voice, chilly with irritation, floated up to the watcher above:

"What's the matter?"

The runner was still puffing, his beefy face showing flushed. "Message from Algar, chief. He's coming in—with the Patrol riding his fins!"

"Patrol!" the man at the keyboard half turned in his chair, his mouth slightly agape.

"Did you warn him that the pull was on?" demanded Rich:

"Sure we did. But he can't evade much longer. He either earths or the Patrol nets him——"

Rich stood very still, his head slightly cocked so that he could see the vision plates. His other assistant, the Rigellian, spoke first:

"Always said we needed a com hook-up down here," he stated, with some of the content of one who is at last proved to be right in a long argument.

The man at the controls had a quick answer for that. "Yes—and how are you going to cut through the interference to hear anything over it?" he began when Rich snapped an order to the messenger:

"Get back up there and tell Jennis to order Algar to go inert at once. In exactly two hours," he was consulting his watch, "we'll off the pull for an hour—an hour, that's all. He's to set down, make the best landing he can under power. It doesn't matter if he smashes the ship—he'll work to save his own skin all right. Then we'll snap on the power and net the Patroller when she comes in for the kill. Get it?"

"Two hours and then off pull—keep it off for one, and he's to make a landing then—then on pull," parroted the messenger. "Got it!"

He turned and pounded out of the room, back into the maze. For a moment Dane longed to be twins so that he might follow that flight and so find the way out of the puzzle. But it was more important now to see how Rich was going to manipulate the installation to neutralize the power for the landing of his subordinate's ship.

"Think he'll make it?" asked the man at the control board.

"Twelve to two he does," snapped the Rigellian. "Algar's a master pilot."

"He'll have to take the pull coming in and be ready to snap on his braking rockets the minute it fades—tricky stuff—" It was plain that the other was dubious.

Rich was still watching the vision plate. Two new lights appeared on its surface. But their fluttering across it was so erratic that Dane, not being briefed on the use of this alien recorder, could make nothing of that weird dance.

Rich's lips were moving, counting off seconds, his eyes going from his watch to the plate and back again. The atmosphere grew more tense. At the control board the man's shoulders were hunched, his attention glued to the row of buttons at his fingertips. While the Rigellian strode with the peculiar gliding walk of his kind to the far end of the wall panel, his scaled, bluish six-fingered hand outstretched to one lever there.

"Wait—!" It was the man at the keyboard. "It's pulsing again——!"

Rich spat a blistering oath. On the screen the dots were moving up and down in a crazy race. And Dane was conscious that the hum of the installation varied, that the beat had developed a tripping accent.

"Get it back!" Rich sped to the keyboard. "Get it back!"

The man showed a face damp with sweat. "How can I?" he demanded. "We don't know why it does this."

"Shorten the beam—that helped once before," that was the Rigellian, of the three he showed the least emotion.

The man pressed two buttons. All three stared at the screen for the results of that move. The wildly flying dots settled down to a pattern not far different from the one they had made when Dane had first come upon the scene.

"How far out does it pull now?" asked Rich.

"Atmosphere level."

"And the ships?"

His underling squinted at the board, consulted some dials. "They won't come into the pull for one—maybe two hours. When we cut like that it takes time to build up the power again. Anyway this doesn't affect that blasted trader any—*she* can't lift."

Rich took a small box from his pocket, poured some of its contents into the palm of his hands and licked it up. "It is pleasant to know that *something* is going right," he observed with a chill in his voice which made Dane's skin prickle.

"We don't know much about this," the man thumbed the edge of the keyboard. "None of us have been trained to use it right. And it was alien made to begin with———"

"Let me know when and if you can get it back on full power again," was all the answer Rich made.

Two hours before they could turn on the full power, Dane thought. Now if in those two hours he and Mura—and maybe Kosti and Ali—could move—that lever the Rigellian had reached for—it must control something important. And if they could

216

take over this room and the men in it, they would learn even more about its operation. Suppose the Patrol ship could make a safe landing on the tail of the outlaw they were pursuing—! What should be *his* next move?

Rich decided it for him. His jaws moving in a rhythmical chewing, the outlaw leader walked toward the hidden door. "You say two hours," he spoke over his shoulder as he went. "It'll be much better all around if you halve that, understand? I'll be back in an hour—be ready to cut in the full beam then." He nodded curtly to the Rigellian and stepped through the opening in the wall.

And this time Dane was ready to follow. He allowed Rich a good start and trailed the other through the winding ways which the outlaw threaded with the ease of much practice. Before they had drawn level with the small beacon provided by Mura's torch, a beacon Rich could not sight from the floor, Dane had the secret of the maze. Two right turns, then one left, and then three right once more, skip the next passage opening and repeat. Rich had made the same pattern four times and Dane was sure that it would continue to carry him to the outer door of the puzzle. But, having learned that, the Trader waited on the wall for the other to work his way five corridors ahead before he crossed to the room where he had left Mura and Ali.

He found Kamil up and walking about now, restored by the steward's first aid. And as Dane climbed down their crude ladder they closed in on him.

"—That's it," he ended his report. "The Patrol's

riding in on this bird's jet stream. As long as they both stay out of the atmosphere they're safe. But once the pull is working full power again—'' he snapped his fingers.

''Our move!'' Kamil got out the words between his swollen lips. ''We've got to cut that power off—totally!''

''Yes,'' Mura crossed to the holds on the wall. ''But first we collect Kosti——''

''How can you get him here? He said he can't walk the walls——''

''A man can do anything if he is forced to it,'' Mura replied. ''You will stay here—I shall bring Kosti. But first show me the route which takes one to this 'heart'——''

Dane climbed the wall behind the steward, led the way across the three intervening spaces to that corridor he had seen Rich traversing. And there he repeated the pattern the outlaw had followed. Mura smiled his placid smile.

''It is very simple, is it not? Now, you wait with Kamil—and do nothing foolish until I return. This is most interesting——''

Dane obediently went back to the room where they had left the engineer-apprentice. Kamil sat on the floor, his back against one of the walls, his battered face turned to the torch light. As Dane's boots hit the pavement he turned his head.

''Welcome aboard,'' he mouthed. ''Now tell me about that installation—'' he went on into a series of questions about what Dane had seen, which sometimes left the cargo-apprentice floundering. Of the machines he had seen little because of their casings.

And he could not describe the control panel very well, having been at the time more intent on the actions of the men by it. He admitted this with some of his old feeling of inadequacy. A Trader kept his eyes open, a Trader had to use both his eyes and his brain at one and the same time. Here he had had another opportunity which he had apparently muffed. And a little of the old antagonism sparked to life inside him.

"What is their source of power?" Ali demanded of the room about them. "We've nothing like it— nothing at all! There must be things here which will put us years ahead—generations——"

"Providing, of course," Dane broke in a little sourly, "that we get to use them. We aren't the winners yet."

"Neither are we licked," Ali retorted.

It was as if their roles had been reversed. Now it was Kamil who was building castles, Dane who did the undermining.

"If Stotz and I could have a couple of hours in that place! By the Black Hole, we did pick a winner when we bid on Limbo——"

Ali seemed able to ignore the fact that Rich was still very much in command of the situation, that the *Queen* was pegged down, and that the enemy had a force which could render their headquarters impenetrable. The more Kamil enlarged on the future to come, the more flaws Dane could see in their actions in the immediate present. But they were both lifted out of their thoughts by a soft hail from above.

"Mura!" Dane jumped to his feet. The steward had been successful in his mission, a second man stood on the wall above, one hand resting on the steward's shoulder.

"Yes," was hissed down at them. "Now it is for you to climb. Up quickly, both of you, time runs out!"

Ali went first, and once or twice he bit off an exclamation as his exertions wrung his sore body. Dane caught up the beacon torch, snapped it off, and went after.

"Now this is what we shall do." Mura was clearly in command, as he had been all the time since they had entered the mountain. "Kosti and Ali shall go by the regular path to the room of the installation. While you and I, Thorson, will take the route along the wall top. They are expecting Rich to return there. Your entrance in his place should surprise them long enough for us to go into action. We must get at that switch and immobilize it. And do whatever else we can to make this devil thing incapable of action in the future. So—now we move——"

They made their way back to the path Rich had used, Kosti walking slowly with his hand on the steward's shoulder, visible shudders shaking his big body. There once more they used the linked belts and lowered the jetman and Ali to the floor of the maze.

The brighter glow of the installation sector was their guide now and they reached the oval wall easily. Mura gestured at Kosti and the jetman raised his voice in the same call the messenger had given earlier. The other three stood tense, ready to move if it worked.

"Salzar!"

Dane's attention was fixed on the Rigellian. The

alien's head went up, his round eyes sought the hidden doorway. It was going to work because that blue hand went to the proper button among the controls. And outside the barrier Kosti stood waiting, his blaster drawn and ready to fire, the unarmed Ali behind him.

17 THE HEART CEASES TO BEAT

As the door slid back into the wall and Kosti leaped through, Mura raised his voice:

"You are covered! Stand where you are!"

The man at the keyboard started, looking over his shoulder at Kosti, his face a mask of wild surprise. But the Rigellian moved with the superhuman speed of his race, his blue hand whipping toward another point on the control board.

It was Dane who fired and struck, not living flesh but that bank of controls. The man at the keyboard screamed, a thin, inhuman cry to echo through the maze. And the Rigellian dropped to the floor. But he was not yet beaten. He threw himself at Kosti, moving with a speed no Terran muscles could equal.

The big man swerved, but not far or fast enough, and went down into a clawing, gouging scramble on the floor. But the other outlaw remained where he was, sounds which bore small likeness to words still bubbling between his lips.

Ali slipped through the door and started around the room, edging with the wall as a support to his weaving legs. He turned his face up to Dane.

"Which is it?" he cried. "That switch——"

"Just ahead—the black one with the device set in the handle," Dane called back. And now the eyes of the man by the keyboard found the two on the top of the wall. Why the sight of them restored his sense they could never know, but his hand went to the weapon at his belt. And at that same instant blaster fire cut so close to him that he must have felt the sear of the beam.

"Your hands—up with your hands—at once!" Mura gave the order with the same snap as Jellico might have used.

The man obeyed, leaning over to plant his outspread fingers on the screen he had watched for so long. But now he was intent upon Ali's tottering advance and on his face there was a growing horror. When Kamil's hand fell on the switch at last he gave another cry.

"Don't!"

But Ali disregarded the warning and pulled the lever down with all his strength. The outlaw at the keyboard screamed for the second time. And there came another answer. The hum which had filled the walls, beat within their bodies for so long, was gone.

The Rigellian wrenched himself free from Kosti's grip and gathered his feet under him to launch himself at the switch. But Ali had flung his whole weight upon the lever, dragging it down until the metal shaft broke off in his hand, determined that it would not be opened again. And at the sight of that the man at the keyboard went mad, flinging himself at Kamil in spite of the menace of Mura's blaster.

Dane had been caught napping, his attention had

been on the Rigellian who, he thought, was the more dangerous of the two. But the steward burned the lunatic down as his tearing hands reached for Ali's throat. The man's shriek was choked in mid cry and he writhed to the floor, on his face. Dane was glad he could not see those blackened features.

The Rigellian got to his feet, his unblinking reptilian eyes fastened on Dane and Mura, very much aware of the two blasters now centered upon him. He pulled his clothing into order and ignored Kosti.

"You have just condemned us all, you know—" his voice speaking the Trade Lingo was flat, unaccented, he might have been exchanging the formal compliments used among his kind.

Kosti moved on him. "Suppose you get your hands up, and don't try the trick your partner pulled——"

The Rigellian shrugged. "There's no need for tricks now. We are all caught in the same trap——"

Ali caught at the chair and lowered himself into it. Behind him the screen was blank—dead.

"And this trap?" asked Mura.

"When you threw that switch and wrecked it—you wrecked all the controls," the Rigellian leaned back against the wall at his ease, no emotion to be read on his scaled face. "We'll never get out of here—in the dark!"

For the first time Dane was aware of a change. The gray radiance which had glowed from the walls of the Forerunners' domain was fading, as the glow might fade from the dying embers of a fire.

"We are locked in," the remorseless voice of

224

their prisoner continued. "And since you've smashed the lock, no one can get us out."

A ray of light answered. The Rigellian showed no interest.

"We don't know all the secrets of this place," he told them. "Wait and see how good your lights will be in here shortly."

Dane turned to the steward. "If we start now— before the light is all gone from the walls——"

The other agreed with a nod and called down to the Rigellian: "Can you open the door?"

His answer came in a detached shake of the alien's head. And Kosti promptly went into action. Using his blaster he burnt holds on the wall. Dane fairly danced in his impatience for them to be out and trying for the entrance, he hated to spare the time for those holds to cool.

But at last they were up and over the wall and all in the road to the outside. In the corridor Kosti pulled the hands of the Rigellian behind him and tied them with the man's own belt before ordering him ahead. Their progress was necessarily slow as even with an aiding hand Ali could not keep a fast pace. And now they were in virtual darkness—the light only a ghostly reflection of the former glow.

Mura snapped on his torch. "We'll use these one at a time. Save the charges for when we need them most."

Dane wondered about that. Torch charges were not easily exhausted, they were made to be in use for months. But the ring of light which guided them now was oddly pallid, grayish, instead of yellow-bright as they expected.

225

"Why not turn it up?" Ali asked after a moment.

There was a snicker out of the gloom from the direction of the Rigellian. Then Mura answered:

"It is up—top strength——"

No one commented, but Dane knew that he was not the only one to watch that faint circle anxiously. And when it faded to a misty light extending hardly a foot beyond, somehow he was not surprised. Kosti, alone, asked a question:

"What's the matter? Wait—!" The beam of his own torch struck out into the thick darkness. For perhaps two minutes it was clear, uncut, and then it, too, began to diminish as if something in the atmosphere sapped it.

"All energy within this space," the Rigellian's voice expounded, "is affected now. There is much of the installation we do not understand. Light goes, and later the air, also——"

Dane drew a long, testing breath. To his mind the chilly atmosphere was the same as it had always been. Perhaps that last embellishment was merely a flight of imagination on the part of their prisoner. But their pace quickened.

The pallid circle of the torch did not fade totally away for some time and they were able to follow the pattern which Rich had betrayed—the one who should guide them out of the labyrinth. There was a vast and brooding silence now that the great machine had stopped and in it the ring of their boots awoke strange echoes. At length Kosti's torch was sucked dry and Dane's pressed into use. They threaded on, from one room to another, down this short corridor to that, trying to make the best possible use of the dying light. But there was no way of gauging how close they were to the outer door.

When the last flicker of Dane's light was in turn swallowed up, Mura gave a new order.

"Now we link ourselves together——"

Dane's right hand clipped into Mura's belt, his left closed about Ali's wrist, providing one link in the chain. And they went on so, a soft murmur of sound telling the cargo-apprentice that the steward in the lead was counting off paces, seeming to have worked out some method of his own for getting them from one unseen point to the next.

But the dark pressed in upon them, thick, tangible, with that odd sensation that darkness on this planet always possessed. It was like pushing through a sluggish fluid and one lost any belief in ground gained, rather there was the feeling of being thrust back for a loss.

Dane followed Mura mechanically, he could only trust that the steward knew what he was doing and that sooner or later he would bring them to the portal of the maze. He himself was panting, as if they had been running, and yet the pace was the unhurried, ground covering stride of the Pool parade ground which they had fallen into insensibly as they advanced in line.

"How many miles do we have to go, anyway?" Kosti's voice arose.

He was answered by another snicker from their prisoner. "What difference does it make, Trader? From this there is no way out—once you smashed that switch."

Did the Rigellian really believe that? If he did why

wasn't he more alarmed himself? Or was he one of those fatalistic races to whom life and death wore much the same face?

There was a surprised grunt from Mura and a second later Dane piled up tight against the steward while Ali and the two following him plowed up in a tangle. To Dane there was only one explanation for that barrier before them—somewhere Mura had miscounted and taken a wrong turn in the dark. They were lost!

"Now where are we?" Kosti asked.

"Lost—" the Rigellian's voice crackled dryly with a cold amusement crisping its tone.

But Dane's hand was on the wall which had brought them up short and now he moved his fingers across its surface. This was not fashioned of the smooth material manufactured by the Forerunners, instead it had the grit of stone. They had reached the native rock of the cave! And Mura confirmed that discovery.

"This is rock—the end of the maze."

"But where's the way out?" persisted Kosti.

"Locked—locked when you broke the switch," the Rigellian replied. "All openings are governed by the installation———"

"If that is so," Ali's voice rose for the first time since they had begun that march, "what happened in the past when you shut off the machine? Were you locked in then until it was turned on once more?"

There was no reply. Then Dane heard a rustle of movement, and queer choking noise, and hard on it the jetman's husky tone:

"When we ask questions, snake man, we get

228

answers! Or take steps. What happened when you shut off that switch before?''

More scuffling sounds. And then a hoarse answer: ''We stayed in here until it was switched on again. It was only off occasionally.''

''It was off for days while Survey was poking about here,'' Dane corrected.

''We didn't come near here then,'' returned the Rigellian promptly—a little too promptly.

''Someone must have stayed in here—to turn it on again when you wanted that done,'' Ali pointed out. ''If the doors were locked you couldn't have gotten in or out——''

''I'm not an engineer,'' the Rigellian had lost some of his detachment, he was sullen.

''No, you're just one of Rich's lieutenants. If there's a way out of here, you'll know it.'' That was Kosti.

''How about your pipe?'' Dane asked Mura whose continued silence puzzled him.

''That I have been trying,'' the steward answered.

''Only it doesn't work, eh? All right, snake man, spill—!'' More sounds of a scuffle and then Ali's voice across them——

''If this is rock, and it is the right place—how about using a blaster?''

To cut through! Dane's hand went to his holster. A blaster could cut rock, cut it with greater dispatch than it had shorn through the tougher material of the maze. The idea struck Kosti too—the muffled noise made by his ''persuasion'' methods ceased.

''You'll have to pick just the right spot,'' Ali continued. ''Where is the door——''

"That can be found by this old snake here, can't it?" purred the jetman.

There was an inarticulate whimper in answer to that. Kosti must have heard it as an assent for he pushed past Dane, shoving the captive before him.

"Right there eh? Well, it better be, blue boy, it just better be!"

Dane nearly lost his balance as the Rigellian was thrust back upon him. He elbowed the man back against the wall and stood waiting.

"That you, Frank? Get back, man—all of you get back!"

A second body was pushed against Dane and he gave ground, retreating with the Rigellian and the other.

"Look out for a back wash, you fool!" Ali called out. "Give it low power 'til you see how that cuts——"

Kosti laughed. "I was flipping a polishing rag, son, when you were learning how to walk. You let the old man show his stuff now. Up ship and out!" With that wild slogan which had resounded in countless bars when the Traders hit dirt after long voyages, blazing light spewed out, blinding them all.

Dane peered between the fingers of a shielding hand and watched that core of brilliance center on the rock, saw the stone glow red and then white before rippling in molten streams to the floor. Heat, waves of roasting heat blasted back at them, forcing retreat for all except that one big figure who stood his ground, pointing the weapon at the rock, his helmet, its protecting visor snapped into place, nodding a little in time with the force bolts which jerked his arm and body as they burst from the weapon in his hand to crash against the disintegrating wall. How could Kosti stand up to that back wash? He was taking more than was possible for a man to endure.

But the beam held steady on the point and the hold grew as stone flaked away in patches, the inner rot spreading. The stink of the discharge filled their throats, gave them hacking coughs, cut at their eyes until tears wet their cheeks. And still Kosti stood in his place, with the stability of a command robot.

"Karl!" Ali's voice rose to a scream, "look out— Let up!"

There was a crash as a piece of rock gave way, bashing down into the corridor of the maze. Just in the last instant the jetman had moved, but he did not give more than the few feet necessary to preserve the minimum safety.

With his free hand he beat at a smoldering patch on his breeches. But his grip on the blaster did not waver and the beam of destruction continued to bore in just where he had aimed it.

By the flame Dane saw the Rigellian's face. His wide eyes centered on Kosti and there was a kind of horror mirrored in them. He edged away from the inferno at the portal, but more as if he feared the man who induced it, than if he were afraid of the blaster work.

"That does it!" Kosti's voice was muffled in his helmet.

As yet they dared not approach the glowing door he had cut for them. But since he had holstered his arm it was plain that he thought the job done. Now he came back to join them, pushing up his visor so by the glow of the cooling rock they could see his face wet and shiny. He pounded vigorously with his gloved hands at places on the front of his tunic and breeches and carried with him the taint of singed leather and fabric.

"What's out there?" Dane wanted to know.

Kosti's nose wrinkled. "Another hallway as black as outer space. But at least we can get out of this whirllyround!"

Impatient as they were to be on their way, they must wait until it was safe to cross that cut which radiated heat. Adjusting helmets, improvising a protection for Ali from the Rigellian's tunic, they made ready. But before they went Kosti gave a last attention to their captive.

"We could pull you through," he observed. "But you might fry on the way, and besides you'd be a dead jet breaking our speed if we tangle with any of your friends outside. So we'll just store you in deep freeze—to be called for." He fastened the man's ankles as well as his wrists and rolled him away from the heated portion of the corridor.

Then with Ali in their midst they hurried through the cut and out into the hall. Darkness closed about them once more, and an experiment proved that here, as well as in the maze, the torches could not fight the blackness. But at least the way before them was smooth and straight and there were no openings along it to betray them into wrong turnings.

They slowed their pace to accommodate Ali, and went linked together by touch as they had in the maze.

"Worm's eye view—" Kosti's grumble came

through the sable quiet. "Did the Forerunners have eyes?"

Dane slipped his arm about the swaying Ali's shoulders and gave him support. He felt the engineer-apprentice wince as his clumsy grasp awoke some bruise to life and adjusted his hold quickly, though Ali made no sound of protest.

"Here is an opening, we have reached the end of this way," Mura said. "Yes, beyond is another passage, wider, much wider——"

"A wider road might lead to a more important section," Dane ventured.

"Just so it gets us out of here!" was Kosti's contribution. "I'm tired of jetting around in this muck hole. Go on, Frank, take us in."

The procession of four moved on, making a sharp turn to the right. They were now marching abreast and Dane had an impression of room about them, though the dark was as complete as ever.

Then they were stopped, not by another barrier but by noise—a shout which exploded along the hall with the crack of a stun rifle. In a moment it was followed by just that—the stun of a rifle.

"Down!" Mura snapped. But the others were already moving.

Dane ducked, pulling Ali with him. Then he was lying flat, trying to sort out some meaning from the wild clamor which floated back to them.

"Small war on—" that was Kosti managing to make himself heard between two bursts of firing.

"And it's coming our way," Ali breathed close to Dane's ear.

The cargo-apprentice drew his blaster, though he

did not see how he was going to make much use of it now. To fire blindly in the dark was not a wise move.

"Yaaaah—" That was no shout of rage, it was the yammering scream of a man who had taken his death wound. And Ali was very right—the battle was fast approaching where they lay.

"Back against the walls," again Mura gave tongue to a move they were already making.

Dane clutched a portion of Ali's torn tunic and felt it rip more as he pulled the engineer-apprentice after him to the right. They fetched up against the wall and stayed there, huddled together and listening.

A flash of light cracked open the curtain about them. Dazzled, Dane had an impression of black forms. And then a smoldering patch of red on the wall was all that marked the burst of a blaster.

"Lord of High Space," Ali half whispered. "If they beam those straight down here, we'll fry!"

Feet pounded toward them and Dane stiffened, clutching his weapon. Maybe he should fire at the sound, knock out the runners before they came too close. But he could not bring himself to squeeze the trigger. All a Trader's ingrained distrust of open battle made him hesitate.

There was light up there now. Not the gray, ghostly gloom which had once lit these halls, but a thick yellow shaft which was both normal and reassuring to Terran eyes. And against that the four from the *Queen* saw five figures take cover on the floor, ready—no longer fleeing, but turning to show their teeth to their pursuers.

18   UP SHIP AND OUT

"SURRENDER! in the name of the Federation—" the voice boomed from the walls about them.

"Patrol!" Ali identified the order.

All right—so the Patrol had landed, Dane was willing to accept that. But which of the parties before them represented law and order? Those waiting attack, or those behind the light, waiting to deliver it?

The light steadily advanced—until one of those in wait shot straight into its heart. There was answering fire through the resulting dark and someone screamed.

If they had any sense, Dane thought, they would now reteat to the maze until the fight was over. This was no time to get caught in a mix-up between Rich's forces and the Patrol. But he made no move to pass that bright thought on to Ali. Instead he found himself leveling his blaster, taking aim through the dark at the roof of the hall in which they lay. He pressed the trigger.

The voltage was still set on 'low' but the beam struck the roof and bit in. And he had not misjudged the distance too badly—that burst of light revealed the men who had shot out the Patrol light—he was sure that the Patrol were the light party now. Their white faces, mouths agape, stared up at the glowing core of destruction over their heads as if they were hypnotized by it. Only one moved, throwing himself back, passing under that coruscating splotch, toward the men from the *Queen*. But he did not get past them.

Kosti launched his body out of the shadows, barely visible in the fading gleam from the roof. He should have struck the fleeing man head on. Instead the other made an unbelievable swift twist of his body which carried him almost by the contact point. Had the jetman's fingers not caught in the fugitive's belt, he would have made it.

Dane fired again, sending a second bolt of fire up beside the first to give Kosti light for his fight. But the flash revealed a far different scene. A figure as tall as the jetman was getting to hands and knees for a second forward dash, while Kosti lay limp and still.

Ali moved, clumsily, but at all the speed he could muster, rolling out so that the other stumbled over his body and went down once more. And then Dane used the blaster for the third time, aiming at a point behind them, bracketing the would-be escapee with the blaze.

"Stop!" again the voice boomed about them. "Stop firing or we'll bring a flamer in and sweep this whole hall!"

A wild beast's snarl from the shadows answered. And at the edge of the last glowing splotch, the one meant to barricade the passage, a dark shape prowled back and forth, its crouching outline suggesting something not human.

Then the light went on again, catching them all in its glare. Nearest to the source of it three outlaws stood, their empty hands rising above their heads. But the beam reached on past them, to reveal Kosti. The big jetman lay still, a trickle of blood on his chin. On the radiance swept, pinpointing Mura as he hurried to Kosti, bringing Ali into focus as he hunched over, clutching at his chest, coughing.

Dane, his back to the glare, was alert, his blaster ready for the next move of that other thing. The thing with slavering lips and slack jaw who prowled up and down at the edge of the burning ring which cut it off from the dark safety beyond, that thing who had once been Salzar, lord of this forgotten kingdom— the thing who had retreated into the Hell of the crax user until it was no longer a man at all!

It turned as the light caught it, snarled and spat at the beam, and then whirled and leaped over the burning area, squalling at the lick of fire, heading for the maze.

"Thorson! Mura!"

Dane shivered. He should be after Salzar but he couldn't force himself to cross those flames to hunt down that thing in the dark. It was with real thankfulness that he heard that sharp call. He looked over his shoulder to its source, but the glare of the light dazzled him and he blinked painfully at the figures advancing around it, able at last to make out the black and silver of the Patrol, the drabber tunics of Trade. He holstered his blaster and waited for them to come up.

It was some time later that he sat at a table in a strange room. A room with furnishings which betrayed the nature of the trap which was Limbo in bald openness, things which had been looted from fifty—a hundred ships—crowded together to provide a tawdry luxury for the private quarters of the man they had known as Salzar Rich.

Dane wolfed down a meal of real food—no concentrates—as he listened half dreamily to Mura deliver a concise report of their activities for the past three days. He fought an aching fatigue which ordered him to put his head down on the table and sleep—just sleep. Instead he sat and chewed on delicacies he had not tasted since he left Terraport.

Black tunics slipped in and out of the room, delivering reports, taking orders from the Squadron Commander who sat with Captain Jellico listening to Mura's often interrupted story. It was rather like the end of a Video serial, decided Dane groggily, all wrapped up in a neat little package. The Patrol had arrived, the situation was now well in hand——

"As nasty a set up as we've ever come across," that was the Patrol officer.

"I take it," Van Rycke observed, "that this is going to clear up a great many disappearances——"

The Patrolman sighed. "We'll have to comb these hills, maybe chop into them, before we have the role complete. Though we can do a lot just listing the loot they gathered in. Yes, it's going to clear a lot of records at Headquarters. Thanks to you, we have the chance to do it." He arose and favored Jellico with a sketch of salute. "My compliments, Captain, if you will be free to join me in about——" he consulted his watch— "three hours, we can have a conference. There are several points to be considered."

He was gone. Dane drank from a mug engraved with the Survey crest. And at the sight of those crossed comets, he shuddered and pushed the container from him. It reminded him too vividly of an earlier discovery. Yes, there should be a wealth of strange relics found here. Somehow he was glad that he did not have the task of sorting out and listing them.

"That maze now," Van Rycke's calm seemed ruffled. "That's worth looking over."

Jellico gave a snort of humorless laughter. "As if the Patrol is going to let anyone but themselves and the Fed experts in there!"

The mention of the maze triggered Dane's memory and for the first time he spoke:

"Rich ran back into that. Have they caught him yet, sir?"

"Not yet," Jellico replied. He did not appear much interested in the problem of the missing outlaw leader. "Crax chewer, isn't he?" Went right over the edge when we caught up with you——"

"Yes, he was insane at the last, sir," Mura agreed. "However, I trust that the Patrol are not discounting him. To hunt a madman through that puzzle without precautions of a most serious kind— that is a task I would not care to assume."

"Well," the Captain got up, "we're not asked to do it. The whole thing's in Patrol hands now, let them worry about it. The sooner we lift ship from this misbegotten place, the better I'll be satisfied. We're Trade, not police.''

''Hmm——'' Van Rycke still lounged in a chair which had been ripped from some liner captain's cabin. ''Yes, Trade—a matter of Trade. We must keep our minds on business.'' But none of Jellico's impatience lurked in his limpid blue eyes. He was bland, and, Dane thought, about to go to work. Van Rycke, Patrol or no Patrol, was not yet through with Limbo.

In spite of Jellico's chaffing to be gone, the Captain did not suggest a return to the *Queen*. Instead he paced warily about the room, stopping now and again to inspect some particular fitting Salzar had fancied enough to have installed there. Van Rycke looked over at Dane and Mura.

''I would suggest,'' he said mildly, ''that you make use of Dr. Rich's bedroom. I think you'll find his bunk soft——''

Still wondering why they were not ordered back to the *Queen* where the injured Kosti and Ali had been sent hours before, Dane followed the steward into the second room of Rich's private suite. Van Rycke had been right about the luxury, but it was no bunk which fronted them, only a wide, real Terra-side bed equipped with self-warming foam blankets and feather down puffs.

Dane shed his helmet, bulky belt, and boots to lie back in the fleecy softness. He was dimly aware of Mura's weight settling down on the other edge of the broad expanse and then he was instantly and deeply asleep.

He was in the control cabin of the *Queen*, it was necessary for him to compute their passage into hyper. And yet across from him sat Salzar Rich, his face disciplined, hard as it had been on that day back on Naxos when they had first met. He, Dane, must get them into hyper, yet if his calculations were wrong Salzar would blast him—and he would fall down, down out of the *Queen* into the maze where something else crouched and yammered in the darkness waiting to hunt him!

Dane's eyes opened, he stared up at a grayness above. His body was shaking with chill, his hands icy cold and wet as he groped for some solid reality among the soft billowy things which melted at his touch. He willed his hands to be still, he dared not even shift his eyes now. There was something here, something which broadcast such a threat of menace that it tore at his nerves.

Dane forced himself to breathe deeply, evenly. Mura was there, but he could not turn his head to make sure— A fraction of an inch at a time he began to shift his position. He had no idea of what he had to face as yet, but fear was there—he could almost taste it, see it as a murky cloud in the air.

He could see the door now, and from beyond he could hear the murmur of voices. Perhaps both the Captain and Van Rycke were still in the outer room. Yes, the door, and now a scrap of the wall by it. His eyes took in a Tri-Dee painting, a vivid landscape from some eerie world, a world dead, sterile to life, and yet in its way beautiful. Now he dared to move his hand, burrowing under those feather-weight covers, striving to arouse Mura, sure that the other

241

would not betray himself, even when waking.

Hand moved, head moved. The picture—and beyond it a strip of woven stuff hanging, glittering with threads which might have been spun of emerald and diamond, a bright, too bright thing which hurt the eyes. And now by that, his shoulders blotting out part of it.

Salzar!

Only an exercise of will such as he had not known he could command kept Dane immovable. Luckily the outlaw was not watching the bed. He was taking a serpent's silent way to the door.

To all outward appearances he was a man again, but there was no sanity in those dark fixed eyes. And in his hands he fondled a weird tube set on an oddly shaped handstock, a thing which must be a weapon. He was gone from in front of the hanging, his head cut the picture. Three feet more and he would be at the door. But the hand Dane had sent to warn Mura was met, enfolded in a warm grasp. He had an ally!

Dane tried to plan the next move. He was on his back, muffled in the thick covers of the bed. It would be impossible to jump Salzar without warning. Yet the outlaw must not be allowed to reach the door and use that weapon.

The hand which Mura had grasped now received a message—it was pushed back toward him forcefully. He hoped that he interpreted that correctly. He tensed and, as a wild cry broke from the throat of his bedmate, Dane rolled over the edge to the floor.

Lightning rent the air, fire burst from the bed. But Dane's hand closed on a strip of Paravian carpet and he gave it a furious tug. Salzar did not lose his

balance, but he fell back against the wall. He swung
the weapon toward the scrambling cargo-apprentice.
Then hands, competent, unhurried, closed about his
throat from behind and dragged him to Van Rycke's
barrel chest as the cargo-master proceeded to sys-
tematically choke him into submission. Dane and
Mura got up from the floor, the blazing bed between
them.

There was more confusion, an eruption of Patrolmen, the removal of Salzar and some hasty fire-
fighting. Dane settled down on a bench with a confirmed distaste for beds. Just let him get back to his
bunk on the *Queen*—that was all he asked. If he
could ever bring himself to try and sleep again.

Van Rycke laid the captured weapon down on the
table. "Something new," he commented. "Perhaps
another Forerunner toy, or maybe just loot. The Feds
can puzzle it out. But at least we know that the dear
doctor is now under control."

"Thanks to you, sir!" Dane gave credit where it
was due.

Van Rycke's brows raised. "I only supplied the
end—there might have been another had we not had
warning. Your voice, I believe, Frank," he nodded
to the steward.

Mura yawned politely behind his hand. His tunic
was hanging open, he had a slightly disheveled air,
but his emotions were all neatly undercover as always.

"A joint enterprise, sir," he returned. "I would
not have been awake to cry out had not Thorson
attended to it. He also delivered the motive power
with the carpet. It is a wonder to me why Salzar

did not burn us first, before he tried to get at you——''

Dane shivered. The smell of the burned bed clothing was strong enough to turn his stomach. He wanted fresh air and lots of it. Also he did *not* want to think of such alternatives as Mura had just spoken about.

''That seals it up,'' Captain Jellico came back into the room followed by the Patrol Commander. ''You've got Rich—what do we do—continue to sit on our fins while you comb the mountains to discover how many ships he smashed up here with that hellish gadget of his?''

''I don't think, Captain, that you will have to stay much longer,'' began the Commander when Van Rycke interrupted.

''Oh, we're in no great hurry. There is the problem of our rights on Limbo. That hasn't been discussed as yet. We have a Survey Auction claim, duly paid for and registered, reinforced by an ''All Rights'' claim good for twelve Terran months. How much these cover salvage and disposal of wrecks found here, and their contents, must be decided——''

''Wrecks as a result of criminal activity,'' began the Commander once more, only to have the cargo-master cut in smoothly for the second time:

''But there were wrecks here before Salzar found the planet. The machine appears to have run erratically since the Forerunners left. Historically speaking there must be a mine of priceless relics buried in the soil of these mountains. Since *those* smashups can not be considered the result of criminal activity, I do not doubt we can advance a very legal claim to them. Our men discovered—and without much of a search—at least two ships which antedate Salzar's arrival here. Two—there may be hundreds—'' he beamed good naturedly at the Commander.

Captain Jellico, listening, lost much of his impatience. He came to sit down beside his cargo-master as if ready to conduct a perfectly normal trade conference.

The Patrolman laughed. ''You're not going to pull *me* into any such squabble, Cargo-master. I can relay your claim and protest to Headquarters—but at the same time I can send you off to quarantine station on Poldar—that's our nearest post—at once—under escort if necessary. I don't think that the Federation is going to turn over any Limbian rights to anyone for some time to come.''

''If they move to cancel contracts made in good faith,'' Van Rycke pointed out, ''they are going to pay for it. In addition there will be Video men on Poldar— And we are not Patrol—your rule of silence does not in any way prevent us from answering questions as to our activities of the past few days. This is colorful news, Commander—in a manner of speaking a legend come to life. 'The Sargasso of Space'—a planet filled with a treasury of long lost ships. The romance of it—'' Van Rycke's eyes half closed, as if he were slightly overcome by the romantic aspects of his own speech. ''You will draw sightseers from all over the Galaxy.''

''Yes,'' Captain Jellico chimed in, ''and they'll come equipped with digging apparatus, too. Van,'' he spoke to the cargo-master, ''this is going to be a *big* thing——''

''How true. Luxury hotels—guided tours—

claims staked out for digging. A fortune—a veritable fortune.''

"No one will land here without official permisson!" The Commander struck back.

"Then I do not envy you the patrol you'll have to keep. How the Video boys will love this story," Van Rycke went back into his daydream. "And," he opened his eyes wide and stared straight at the Commander, "you needn't have any thoughts about putting us in cold storage either. We shall appeal to Trade in hyper code—that you can't jam."

The Patrolman appeared hurt. "Have we given you any indication that we intend to treat you as criminals?"

"Not at all—just some hints here and there. Oh, we'll go off to quarantine like the good, honest, law-abiding Galactic citizens that we are. But as good, honest law-abiding citizens we shall also tell our story far and wide—unless some adequate arrangements may be made."

The Commander came directly to the point: "And what is your idea of an 'adequate arrangement'?"

"Suitable reparation for our loss of claims here—along with reward money."

"What reward?"

Van Ryke ticked points off on his fingers. "You landed here intact because men from the *Queen* had turned off that installation. The same party from our ship discovered the *Rimbold*, I believe you have been feverishly seeking her for some time now. And we also delivered Salzar to you, neatly done up in a package. I can undoubtedly make other additions to this list——"

Once more the Patrolman laughed. "Who am I to argue with a Trader over his proper profit? I'll post your claim at headquarters if you promise to hold your collective tongues at quarantine——"

"For a week," Van Rycke answered. "Just seven Terran days. Then Video shall have the story of our lives. So tell your big brass to get moving. We'll lift today—or rather tonight— And we'll go to Poldar. Also we shall notify Trade just where we are and how *long* we shall be there."

"I'll let you fight it out with the big boys." The Commander sounded resigned. "I have your word you'll go directly to Poldar?"

Captain Jellico nodded. "You need not send for an escort. Good hunting, Commander."

Dane and Mura followed their officers out of the room, but the cargo-apprentice was troubled. To be shut up in a Patrol quarantine station was the usual result of a flight to a new and unknown planet. There would be all the poking and prying of doctors and scientists to make sure that neither men nor ship had brought back any deadly disease. But this had over-tones of a longer imprisonment. Yet neither the Captain nor Van Rycke appeared in the least cast-down. In fact they were at peace with their world as they had not been since that auction on Naxos.

"Have something in mind, Van?" Jellico's voice could be heard above the rumble of the crawler taking them back to the *Queen.*

"I looked over Salzar's loot pretty carefully. Remember Traxt Cam, Captain?"

"Traxt Cam—he operates out on the Rim——"

"Operated," Van Rycke's voice lost some of its lightness.

"You mean he was one of Salzar's victims?"

"I don't see how else his private record box got in Salzar's general catch. Traxt was on his way in from a very good thing when he smashed here. He'd bid for Sargol. Got it, and was doing all right there——"

"Sargol," repeated the Captain. "Sargol—isn't that planet where they found the Koros—the new jewels?"

"Yes. And Traxt's claim has a year and a half yet to go. We shall point that out to the powers that be. They might well be ready to settle with us even—our Limbo papers turned in without any back chat from us—a full shipment of supplies for the *Queen*—and the rest of Traxt's claim to exploit. How does it sound, Captain?"

"Just like one of your better deals, Van. Yes, the big boys might go for that. It would cost them little and get us out of their hair—put us out on the Rim where we can't talk too much—"

"Might work?" Van Rycke shook his head solemnly. "Captain, give me more credit. Of course it *will* work. Sargol and the Koros—they're waiting for us."

His confidence built a feeling of security. Dane stared out over the bare bones of Limbo without seeing that seared waste, he was trying so hard to picture Sargol. A mining planet with a rich strike and the *Queen*'s Trade claims paramount! Maybe Limbo had brought them luck after all. They'd be able to answer that better in a month or two.

ISAAC ASIMOV

37416	**Is Anyone There?**	$1.50
41661	**Jupiter**	$1.75
*52220	**Of Matters Great and Small** $1.95	
63120	**Only A Trillion**	$1.50
*75456	**Science, Numbers and I**	$1.50
*78456	**The Stars In Their Courses** $1.50	
83226	**Twentieth Century Discovery** $1.50	

ALL TWELVE TITLES AVAILABLE FROM ACE
$1.95 EACH

_____ 11671 CONAN, #1
_____ 11672 CONAN OF CIMMERIA, #2
_____ 11673 CONAN THE FREEBOOTER, #3
_____ 11674 CONAN THE WANDERER, #4
_____ 11675 CONAN THE ADVENTURER, #5
_____ 11676 CONAN THE BUCCANEER, #6
_____ 11677 CONAN THE WARRIOR, #7
_____ 11678 CONAN THE USURPER, #8
_____ 11679 CONAN THE CONQUEROR, #9
_____ 11680 CONAN THE AVENGER, #10
_____ 11682 CONAN OF AQUILONIA, #11
_____ 11681 CONAN OF THE ISLES, #12

AVAILABLE WHERE PAPERBACKS ARE
SOLD OR USE THIS COUPON

- - - - - - - - - - - - - - - - - -

ace books, (Dept. MM) Box 576, Times Square Station
New York, N.Y. 10036

Please send me titles checked above.

I enclose $ _____ Add 35c handling fee per copy.

Name _____

Address _____

City _____ State _____ Zip _____

73

There are a lot more
where this one came from!

ORDER your FREE catalog of ACE paperbacks here. We have hundreds of inexpensive
books where this one came from priced from
75¢ to $2.50. Now you can read all the books
you have always wanted to at tremendous
savings. Order your *free* catalog of ACE
paperbacks now.

CE BOOKS ● Box 576, Times Square Station ● New York, N.Y. 10036